I0653822

THE MADDY SAGA

BOOK ELEVEN

PONYGIRL'S CHOICE

BY

PAUL BLADES

Cover Art by Amy Row
amyrow.com

Copyright©2012 Paul Blades

Dark Visions Publications
darkvisionspub@gmail.com

Other Books by Paul Blades:

The Blue Cantina- Books I and II
Klitzman's Isle
Klitzman's empire
Klitzman's Paradise
Klitzman's Pawn- Parts One and Two
Slaver's Dozen- A Tale of Klitzman's Isle
Klitzman's Predators
Three by Blades
The Taking of Cheryl Parts One and Two
Sacrifice to the Emerald God
The Warlord's Concubine, Books 1, 2, 3, & 4
Dreams and Desires, Books One and Two
Carmella Condemned
Carmella's Fate
The Seduction of Morningstar Bridges

The Maddy Saga:

Vol. I	Maddy becomes a Ponygirl
Vol. II	The Training of a Ponygirl
Vol. III	Ponygirl Champion
Vol. IV	Ponygirl Summer
Vol. V	Ponygirl Love
Vol. VI	Ponygirl Season
Vol. VII	Ponygirl Gambit
Vol. VIII	Ponygirl Pleasures
Vol. IX	Ponygirl Peril
Vol. X	Ponygirl's Fate
Vol. XI	Ponygirl's Choice

CHAPTER ONE

Sitting in the Strelnikov box with the family and Irkut while they waited for the next race to begin the morning after his night of orgy with the four blond women, Jake's recollections of their night of pleasure made the gentle jibes and teasing of the women more piquant. As he looked at the slender Lada, he recalled her small, firm breasts in his mouth. He recalled the doctor's tortuous possession of his tool in between her lips, Zoya's exuberant encouragement for him to fill her with his cum. Most of all, he remembered Tanya's happy, pleased face when he emerged from between Lada's teenaged thighs.

Both Helena and Vassily, too, seemed pleased at the happiness of their friend and daughters. Vassily kept giving him knowing grins and Helena kept dropping hints that she deserved her own turn with the wiry, muscular American.

The next race was the Troika Championship. Grobgy had a team in this race as well. If they won this one, his estate was a cinch for the Estate Championship again this fall. Only one other estate had won both the spring and fall championships in one year, about eight years before, while the sport was just beginning to expand to its current level. It would be a feather in Grobgy's cap.

The two teams of three pony carts were taking their warm up laps. Unlike during the earlier rounds when there were so many races to run, in the championship round, the ponies were afforded ample opportunity to loosen their legs and shoulder muscles on the track. It was the green team against Grobgy's blue and gold one.

"Who do you like," Tanya asked Irkut, considered the expert on all things ponygirl related.

"I like Jake," Lada said, giggling. "But I think he may need more training. What do you say, Jake, would you like another workout?"

"I think he needs a more experienced trainer to show him the ropes," Helena said, a broad grin over her face.

Irkut had not been let in on the not so secret secret of Jake's multiple liaison of the night before, but he had made a very educated guess based on the way the women were constantly smiling at his American friend and touching and petting him every chance they got. "There's no substitute for experience, eh, Vassily," he joked.

Vassily smiled and rubbed his hand over his attractive, vivacious wife's thigh. "An experienced trainer will really put you through the ropes," he said, laughing. "You need stamina above all else."

Zoya's shoeless foot was running up and down Jake's calf. "I think Jake has the stamina, Papa. And he's very good at the finish." Even Jake had to laugh at this one.

Finally responding to Tanya's earnest and innocent question, Irkut pointed out why he gave Grobgy's team the edge. "Although the green team was seeded one higher than the Grobgy team, number three to their four, Grobgy's team has been running longer together, three seasons, I believe. They also defeated the number one and two seeds during the qualifying matches yesterday and the day before. While the green team bested the number two seed, it lost to the number one, which would be in the finals were it not for one of its ponies catching her boot in a rut. The five seconds it took to recover top speed cost them the race and the tournament."

"But didn't the green team have a better record during the season?" Jake asked looking over the program. "They won eleven out of fourteen to Grobgy's team's nine."

"But look who they ran against," Irkut pointed out. "Only two of the teams that the green team defeated made it to the tournament. And the green team's times were weak yesterday. I'm going with Grobgy's team on this one."

"I'm sorry," Jake said. "I can't bring myself to bet on Grobgy's ponies. I know that I'm betting with my heart and not my head, but I'm going for the green team."

"You better go and get your bets in," Helena said. "They're about to start." As a driver, Helena was forbidden to bet on the ponygirls. Although it was a rule mostly honored in its breech, Helena was a stickler for rules.

Tanya said that she would go with Jake's pick and handed him a fifty zlotski note to put down for her. The others begged off.

Irkut and Jake went up to the ticket booths on the level above the Strelnikov box. There was a long line. Ahead of them was a delicious looking, brown haired slave girl. She wasn't placing a bet for herself, of course, but her owner had written out a betting slip and placed it into a pouch around her neck together with his bet. The girl, gagged and with her hands bound behind her, merely had to present the pouch to the ticket clerk and he would put the ducat in the pouch for return to her master. Despite his sexual satisfaction from the night before, Jake had to admire the girl's firm derrière as she made little hops up and down, anxious lest she not get the bet down before the ponies went off. There was a minute and a half to go and three bettors ahead of her.

She made it with enough time to spare so that Jake and Irkut could get their bets down as well. When she turned to run back to her master, Jake saw the name, 'Linda', etched in blue across her upper chest and Burnham's fierce, black mastiff tattooed on her belly. She was one of Burnham's early trainees who had passed into the hands of an ultimate buyer. A dark shadow passed over him as he thought of the perfidious billionaire and the role that he himself had had in bringing the lovely, innocent looking, American girl to Kalikastan. When Irkut handed him his betting slip, he smiled, determined not to let anything darken his day.

Irkut, who had made a bundle from the earlier races, had gotten this one wrong. The green team, three beautiful, dark skinned ponies, one Italian, one Spaniard and one Greek, took the lead at the 3/4 pole and never gave it back.

Irkut tore up his ducat and tossed it into the air. "That's why they call it gambling," he said. Jake was pleased at the Grobgy estate defeat.

The yearling final was next. It would be followed by Chocolate's race, the 1500 sulky, and then Lightning in the 3000. That would be the end of the official tournament. Jake was so anxious for the races to go, he could not sit still. While the yearlings were lining up, he watched Chocolate in the paddock with his binoculars. She looked fit, she looked ready. She had to race the number 2 pony, the one who had gallantly allowed her to stay in the tournament by, in essence, throwing its race. Not that the pony had anything to do with it. The pony probably wondered why they were standing there a few feet away from the finish line and waiting for the brown skinned pony to pass them. Perhaps it would never know. What business was it of a ponygirl anyway?

Chocolate was nervously shifting from booted foot to booted foot down in the paddock. She realized that this was the championship race, the one she must win to get to the ultimate race. She could tell by the excitement of the crowd and the nervousness of her driver earlier. His slave girl had been tormenting her sex all day, raising her lusts to a fevered pitch and then denying them. The numerous completions she had been permitted right after her injury were a thing of the past.

There had been something about the blond haired woman who had cared for her that Chocolate liked. Her hands had been friendly and knowing. She wore a pretty smile almost all the time and seemed utterly content with her life. Since people didn't speak to ponygirls, much of their understanding about what was going on around them had to come from reading people's faces, gauging their moods. Chocolate liked the lady even though she had whipped her breasts yesterday before her first race. The lady had kissed both her nipples afterwards as if reassuring the pony that now that the necessary had been performed, their relationship could go on as before.

The ponygirl had been on edge as her driver's slave girl harnessed her for the race about an hour earlier. Chocolate could see that the girl was nervous too. She fumbled with some of the straps and had to redo them. Chocolate thought that she saw a tear in the girl's eye. Her heart went out to the ever naked, blond haired, young woman. While she, Chocolate, would, hopefully, be transformed back into Jackie the, hopefully, former Chicago whore, the girl would remain a slave girl probably forever. Chocolate did not know how she could deal with it if she thought that her present fate was permanent.

Chocolate realized that she had the keys to another pony's freedom in her legs. She often thought of the poor girl, Maddy. How awful must it have been to be kidnapped and not knowing what fate had in store for you, and then to wake up here, a strange country where ordinary morality seemed to have been stood on its ear. At least she had known what was happening when the men came for her. She knew that she was going to be a ponygirl and, mostly, what that pertained. Even then it had been horrible, much worse than she had expected even though Jake had explained it all to her in advance.

Now, redemption was at hand. And she was in line to be a champion at long last. She hoped that Jake could arrange it so that, if she did win a championship medal, she could take it home with her when they left. It would be fun to have it on her mantelpiece in her Malibu beach house and have no one but her, and Jake when he came to visit, he would always be welcome, know what it was.

Her driver looked resplendent when he emerged form the trailer dressed in his racing uniform. It was quartered in black and gold like her hood. His boots were shiny. She would have, she hoped, at least one more session with his wonderful cock before she was liberated.

Giorgi stepped up to the pony. He intuited that she was aware of the importance of this race. A smart ponygirl driver does not underestimate the intelligence of his animal. They may be silent and physically helpless, unfamiliar with the mostly Russian spoken around them, but they are acute observers. After all, they have nothing else to do. They can also discern a driver's emotion, taking confidence when the driver exuded it, losing it when the driver seemed hesitant and doubtful.

Right now, Giorgi was trying to show his most confident best. He was worried though. The pony had been lucky yesterday that she had not been required to run against the number 3 seed pony in her last race. Chocolate still limped and, when her leg was massaged, it was still sore. An ugly black and blue mark ran from just below her hip to her knee. He had had her down at the track early this morning working on starts and on that important second step which often determined which pony commanded the early lead, she was kind of hesitant. Maybe it would be different during the race itself. Ponygirls weren't stupid and they knew the difference between a practice run and a race. While they would not be deliberately disobedient, they would interpret orders most favorably to themselves when they wanted or had to. So the orders to start during their practice runs this morning were interpreted as start, but don't hurt yourself.

Jake and Irkut had come by that morning to wish Giorgi luck. Burnham had come too, at a different time. He did not like the wealthy American. He did like his money though and there was a big bonus due for winning the championship. Usually there was a sliding scale for bonuses depending how far one got in a tournament, so much for making the tournament at all, so much for second, third or fourth place. The other places didn't matter. But Burnham had made it clear that he cared only about first place. He eliminated all the bonuses in their agreement except the one for winning, which he tripled. At the end of today, Giorgi could be very well off indeed.

He ran his small but powerful right hand over the pony's left outer thigh. What strength he felt there! What a beautiful creature she was, so much like a woman, but yet bestial. Her belly flinched slightly as he ran his hand across it, obscuring temporarily the fierce black headed mastiff tattooed there. She spread her thighs obediently when he placed his palm over her pudenda and caressed it softly. He would not put false confidence on in front of the proud pony. She had worked too hard, given him too much for that. He looked her in her eyes, through the tiny portals of her hood, at the face he had never seen and never would. He knew that she could win. He wanted her to know that. He also wanted her to know that it would be hard, that it would take all that she had. She would need to be willing to run herself into the ground to become a champion today.

He sensed an understanding of his message coming from the pony. Her posture grew a little bit straighter, her muscles just a little bit firmer as if readying themselves for their ordeal to come. He stood on his tip toes and took the pony's right teat in his mouth while circling the breast with his hand. He gave it a long, sensuous kiss. He did the same on the left. Their fates were tied together; he wanted the pony to know that. He would do the best he could for her if she would do the best for him.

When he was finished, he bound and gagged his slave girl, donned his racing cap, and then hopped up onto the sulky seat.

Chocolate's beautiful, brown body trilled with sexual need as she pulled the sulky cart down to the tournament track. She was amazed that the crowds in the stands seemed even larger than the previous days. Fans lined the rails calling her name in Russian, *Shokoladniy! Shokoladniy! Shokoladniy!* The pony had lost her consciousness of her nakedness, for the most part, long ago, having accepted her transformation into another kind of creature, albeit temporarily. Her heart surged when she heard her name called. High school track had been nothing like this! She proudly pulled her cart around the track to the paddock area. There, she waited anxiously for the race before hers to finish before she could take her place on the track itself.

She heard the gun for the prior race go off and the crowd cheer. Standing not more than fifteen feet away from her was her adversary. Chocolate admired her firm, thick thighs, her taut belly and her broad, strong shoulders. She was a natural ponygirl, something that Chocolate would not have recognized at all five months ago. Her skin was pale and her ponytail black. She was wearing a red and green hood. Chocolate recognized her as the pony that had been held back so that she could win the race the day before yesterday. The pony had been fast and had pulled ahead of her at an alarming rate. Chocolate recognized that she would have to work hard.

Vixen, Chocolate's Alsatian opponent, eyed the brown skinned pony warily. She saw Chocolate's thick, firm, thigh muscles and her powerful shoulders. She too knew that this race would be a hard one. Her pussy, too, vibrated with the need for completion, as she had been teased and stroked much like Chocolate had. This was her third tournament and the first time she had made the finals. She had been beaten severely each time she had lost before and she expected no less now. She wanted to avoid that beating at all costs and, instead, to enjoy the privilege of the pleasure her diminutive driver's cock could bring her. Long gone were any thoughts of her days as a French University student, long gone were any thoughts of that boy who had loved her back in Rheims. She had been a ponygirl for two years and knew that she would never be anything else. But to be a champion! That was something that they could never take away from her. She wanted one of those golden medals hanging from her collar. Most of all, right now, she wanted a stiff cock between her legs to assuage her burning lust. There was only one way to get one and that was victory.

The prior race finished and both Chocolate, wearing her black and gold hood, and Vixen, wearing her green and red one pulled out onto the track for their warm up laps. Isolated calls of *Shokoladniy!* or *Viksen!* could be heard from the crowd. This was one of the races that everyone had been waiting to see. Those who had missed Vixen's driver's noble gesture of the other day had made certain that they would be in the stands for this race. Betting was heavy. Those that knew ponygirl racing knew that Chocolate had not been severely tested since her injury and so the smart money was on Vixen at 5 to 2. The emotional favorite of the crowd was Chocolate and that's where the money of the hoi polloi went.

After an easy cruise around the track, the two ponies sidled up to the start line. The excited crowd drew to a hush while the starter put his pistol into the air. He called out, "One, two…" and on the beat of three, he fired the pistol.

Giorgi knew that Chocolate had it in her. At his signal, she pushed off mightily with her uninjured right foot and extended her mighty left one forwards as far as it would go. Her boot dug into the loose, dirt track and she gave a powerful thrust, just like they had practiced it a thousand times before.

The ponies were off to a nearly identical start. There are no films of the race, because those things just aren't done for security reasons, but if there was one, it would have shown two ponies furiously churning their knees in the air, their large breasts weaving and bouncing, sweat pouring off their frames, going virtually exactly dead even the whole 1500 meters.

First, Chocolate gained a few inches on her rival, the top of her head jutting past the plane which would have measured the beginning of Vixen's. Then, at the quarter mile, Vixen had a slight lead, perhaps seven or eight inches. Each pony was pouring its heart into the race. The drivers were slashing their whips and yelling frantically for more speed.

Giorgi was at his wit's end. Each time that Chocolate sped up, the Alsatian pony sped up too, a mere second later. Happily, when the Alsatian found an extra burst of speed, Chocolate was able to dig down inside her and find some too.

Up in the stands, Irkut, Jake and 8,972 people, not including about 950 slave girls, assorted trainers and drivers who were hanging about to watch what might be history, vendors, maintenance workers, pickpockets, con men, hustlers and touts, all rose to their feet and started to cheer. Irkut leaned over to Jake and shouted above the noise, "They're going too fast! One of them's going to break!"

Jake heard Irkut's voice, but not his words. "Come on Chocolate! Come on Chocolate! Come on Chocolate!" he was yelling at the top of his lungs. Tanya was jumping up and down beside him, a wild grin on her face. Helena and Vassily, experts like Irkut, peered unbelievingly out at the two speeding ponies, knowing what they were risking and knowing what this kind of a race might do to Chocolate's injury. They, like all the others in the Strelnikov box, had placed their money on Chocolate. But their concern was not for their money, it was for the welfare of two, beautiful specimens of ponygirl and their new friends, Jake and Irkut, who had so much riding on Chocolate's victory.

Chocolate could not believe the pace of the race. She had run fast before, but not like this. By the half way mark, each long stride caused her tendons and muscles to scream, her lungs to beg for more air. It was like a 100 meter dash done 150 times.

Burnham, up in the owner's box was silently shouting in his own head, his binoculars pinned to his forehead. "Come on Chocolate! You can do it! You can do it!"

The slave girl, Orchid, who had been busy earlier this afternoon servicing some of Burnham's new found friends, but who had been on her owner's lap, her torso over his knee, her legs spread, her master's unconscionable hand in her tired, sore, squishy quim, fell to the floor as he rose. The shouts and screams of the people around her were frightening. "What kind of a place have they brought me to?" she wondered fearfully. "Have they all gone mad?"

By the time that the ponies reached the ¾ pole, everyone could tell that they were tiring. Their bare chests were bright red and their cheeks puffed in and out, accommodating the huge drafts of air they needed to keep going. It was record time at the ¾ pole, but it was difficult to see who was in the lead. Chocolate had the outside rail as befitted her lower seed and her body blocked the view of almost everyone.

The standing room only crowd pressed against the rails, everyone anxious to be an eyewitness to the ponies crossing the finish line. There was no chanting, just over 9,000 voices independently shouting out the name of their choice for champion. After the race, the emergency crews had to be summoned to treat several cases of crushed ribs of people jammed up against the rail and one heart attack, non-fatal.

As they came around the near turn and broke into the straightaway that led to the finish line, the two ponies were still neck and neck. Giorgi had thrown away his whip and was practically standing in his seat, screaming maniacally in Russian, "Faster! Faster! Faster!" The other driver was doing the same.

Some said later that it was too good a race to ever end. That if it was a perfect world, the two paragons of ponygirl beauty, strength, speed and heart, would still be racing and would race each other, preserving that virtually sacred six minutes, till the end of time.

Although either pony's overall time would have set a new tournament and world record in the 1500 meter sulky race, you would not have known it by the last 200 meters. Both ponies had slowed down appreciably although their efforts to draw out one more tiny ounce of reserve had not. 150, 100, 75, 50 meters and the ponies were still dead even. And then something happened which often determines which pony will be recalled until the end of time and which will be a footnote. The Alsatian had an apparent six or seven inch lead. All she had to do was keep putting one booted foot in front of another. In an effort to add to her stride, however, some 15 meters from the finish, she overextended her right leg by just a few centimeters, lost her balance, and crossed the finish line in a pronounced stumble. Chocolate maintained her pace, and the minute reduction in speed of Vixen, the beautiful, Alsatian ponygirl, gave her the opportunity to gain the ten inches she needed for a clear victory.

Those few people directly on the finish line saw it quite clearly. Those to the left and behind the ponies, saw Vixen as the first finisher. Those to the right, had an equally distorted view and were certain that Chocolate had a wide margin of at least two feet. The official results were delayed by the need to confirm Chocolate's victory via a photo finish shoot.

As the ponies crossed the finish line, the crowd issued a loud groan of unhappiness as it watched Vixen, unable to regain its balance, fall to the ground. Giorgi, not knowing what had happened, but hearing the noise, looked back. Virtually every eye was on the poor Alsatian pony as its torso dragged in its reins while its feet tried vainly to reacquire stability. Two pairs of eyes were on Chocolate, though. One, her trainer, the one charged with winning everything, including the all important race the next day, inhaled sharply with concern. The other, a black suited ponygirl trainer who was responsible for developing last year's 1500 meter champion and, quite possibly, this year's 3000, gave out a short shout of glee which was overwhelmed by the noise of the crowd around him.

For as Chocolate responded to her driver's automatic pull back of her reins to signal her to slow down to a walking pace, she gave a little hop with her left leg. She did it twice more and then resumed her normal gait. Chocolate had aggravated her injury.

For the moment, all concerns about Chocolate's injury went by the boards. The tall, broad shouldered, dark skinned pony was jubilant. She had done it! She had really done it! All those months of cruel, harsh training, all that she had suffered, all seemed to slip away as the magnitude of her achievement came home to her. She happily trotted around the track in her victory lap as the announcer relayed to the crowd the irrefutable verdict of the flash photo taken at the moment of victory. The crowd was ecstatic in its celebration. Even the losing betters were carried away with the fairy tale ending.

Chocolate's blood was still up as she was directed to the winner's circle by her happy driver. The racing officials, including the President of the Racing Commission, were waiting there. Races like Chocolate's were good for the sport and they were all very pleased. Burnham came rushing in to claim his trophy. Jake and Irkut came down from the stands, Tanya at Jake's side, to give their congratulations. A huge garland of pink, yellow, and blue flowers was draped around Chocolate's neck. The ceremony was short and sweet. After the tall, silver trophy, its top crowned with a statuette of a ponygirl, was presented to Burnham, the President of the Racing Commission attached a golden medal to Chocolate's collar, the emblem of a ponygirl champion. Chocolate felt a thrill run through her body when she felt it dangling there. She had finally, after all those years, won the top prize.

All, except Tanya, posed for the obligatory picture. Giorgi stood to the left of the harnessed ponygirl, Burnham to its right. Irkut, the pony's trainer stood next to Giorgi and Jake stood next to Burnham. The picture was not for widespread dissemination, of course. People outside of Kalikastan might not understand the esthetic beauties of the national sport. Only two copies would be made. The first would adorn a wall in the enclosed owners' clubhouse. The second would be given to Chocolate's owner, Burnham, so that he could hang it on a wall in his mansion. It is the only known photograph of Jake in that country and only one among maybe four or five known grainy, hurried photos of him anywhere.

A crowd of admirers surrounded and pressed in on them. Chocolate felt more than one hand reaching out to touch her sweaty skin. When the picture taking was over, the crowd dispersed and Giorgi hopped onto the cart to drive the pony back to the encampment. "Is this all there is?" Jake thought as he watched the ponycart recede. Undoubtedly, the fact that the true championship would not be determined until tomorrow had detracted from the celebration. Burnham went back to the owner's clubhouse, his trophy in hand. Jake and Tanya went back up into her family's box to await the next and final race of the day, the 3000 meter sulky, Lightning's race.

Lightning, although she heard the commotion of the crowd at the conclusion of Chocolate's race, was totally oblivious to its importance to her. She was waiting in the paddock area, fixed into her traces, nervously shifting her weight between her black booted feet. She knew that this was the championship race of her division. Her driver had impressed on her the importance of this race much like he had the importance of the championship race in the Spring Tournament. He had her kneel down in front of him while his slave girl encouraged his cock to completion with her mouth and hands. When his eruption occurred, he took charge of his prick and directed his discharge into Lightning's poised mouth. It was a reminder to her that the route to sexual satisfaction was through victory.

Lightning could still taste the faint remnants of his tart fluids as she waited to be driven out onto the track for her warm up runs. The leather encased, steel bit in her mouth was held tightly against her teeth and its prong rested on her tongue. Her driver was pacing back and forth nervously and Lightning, even though she had been forbidden speech for almost nine months now, had the urge to tell him to go sit in the sulky carriage because he was spreading his worry and uncertainty regarding the outcome of the upcoming race to her.

The physician had come by this morning and examined her foot. All that Lightning knew was that he had frowned and then rebandaged it. She had heard the men talking in their rough and, to her, strange dialect, and saw her owner, the large, black bearded man, and her trainer arguing, she assumed, about whether she was capable of running or not. Her owner, of course, won.

As far as Lightning was concerned, her foot was fine. It hurt when she walked on it and it had been very sore last night after she had finished her semi final round. But it had been iced immediately and the soothing salve the doctor had given to her driver applied. This morning, the acute pain was gone. Lightning knew that it would return once she applied the stress of the race track to it, but she was sure that her determination to be a repeat champion would see her way past the pain.

As she waited for the order to proceed to the track, standing motionless in the paddock, Lightning bristled as the surrounding host of onlookers prattled and pointed at her and her adversary, two fine specimens of female anatomy, bared but for their confining and utilitarian harnesses. Seven times in the last three days, she had stood here, the object of scrutiny of the bettors and punters, the dedicated fans of the sport and the merely curious. Through her little apertures on the world, the small dime sized holes in her blue and gold hood over her eyes, she saw the women who came to gawk. They ranged from young to old and their dress ranged from the opulent to scanty.

Lightning had long ago gotten used to being naked to the world. She could not help be reminded, however, of her own former life as a young woman each time she was exposed in close quarters to the gay and carefree young women in the crowd who came to see her. Normally, she put away thoughts of her human past, even on race days. But the tournaments brought out a raucous, energetic crowd, especially in the championship rounds. It was at times like these that the events that had propelled her here seemed so unreal, as if she could turn to her driver, inform him of her decision to return to human life and walk away. The reality of the straps that kept her wrists perpetually fastened behind her, the hood that obscured her human features, the hard, cruel bit she carried in her mouth, were all reminders that she was not in some dream, that this was not just some weird costume drama that she was engaged in.

Lightning cast a glance at the other pony, her opponent. She was wearing a green and blue hood. She looked strong and fit. One of them today would be rewarded for their championship with a round of carnal delight administered by her driver, her owner and other, unknown men. The other would be whipped to within an inch of her life. Victory was all. Second place, for all practical purposes, did not exist. She had no desire to suffer the cruel whipping that would be prompted by failure. If only her victory did not portend hellish torture for the other pony, she could look forward to her victory without a tinge of guilt. Her escape from torment would seal the other pony's doom and vice versa.

The other pony seemed calm and ready for the upcoming test of speed and endurance. She had fine, round breasts and a dark shade of skin. Her tail was black as it protruded from her hood and reached down to the middle of her shoulder blades. She stood about fifteen feet to Lightning's left. Her driver too was pacing back and forth, awaiting the signal from the track officials that it was time to mount up. He was a mite taller than her driver, but seemed thinner, almost wiry. Lightning could not help but wonder if life under his tutelage was as harsh and painful as life under hers.

She wondered too, about where the other pony was from. Was she Hispanic? American perhaps? Mediterranean? She almost certainly rued the day of her capture as much as she did, yearning for a chance to go back in time and change events. But even if she was brought back in time with the knowledge of the harsh destiny that threatened her, what would she change? Lightning didn't know how the people who had kidnapped her had selected her from the hundreds of thousands of women her age across the country. If she had, for instance, cut class on the night of her kidnapping many months ago, wouldn't her kidnappers have merely devised some other plan for apprehending her? She would have to live her life in constant fear of the unknown. Many times she had racked her brains to see if she could remember having had contact with either of her kidnappers before the night they grabbed her. It had been to no avail. It all seemed so random and arbitrary, so unjust.

The drivers had apparently received the signal to mount their sulky carts. Her driver paused momentarily to stroke her hairless quim for good luck and then went and swung himself up into his seat. Lightning stood poised to receive his signal to move. It would be a grievous error to move even an inch before her driver gave the command. She felt the flick on her reins that meant proceed slowly, and she began to tow her burden forwards.

The crowd around the paddock took the movement of the two ponies as a signal to call out the names of their favorites. Lightning heard her name called out by several of the onlookers interspersed with strange words that she could not understand. She took them as a wish for good luck; but luck would have little to do with which pony would emerge victorious. Sometimes it happened, a pony stepped in a hole or slipped on a wet spot that had not been covered with sand by the grooms. Sometimes a belt slipped or a wheel froze up. But these occasions were rare. Strength and speed, that was what would determine which of them would be fucked beyond sensibility and which would suffer the whip.

The other pony entered the track area first, as befitted the challenger. She was a Rumanian female, swept up off of the streets of Bucharest one night. She had been a pony three years and this was the furthest she had ever advanced in her five previous tournaments. Her name was Gypsy, appropriate to her origins. Lightning followed, as was proper for the higher seeded pony.

The crowd roared when the two ponies came out onto the track. It was the last race of the day and the people were ready to let loose all their inhibitions. Lightning's driver waited until the other pony had pulled many lengths ahead before he started Lightning into her warm up trot. It was common courtesy to allow the other pony to warm up at her own pace without concern for being shown up by her competitor. The real competition would begin soon enough.

It felt good to Lightning to have the soft dirt of the track beneath her feet at last. Her driver let her trot slowly for about two minutes before urging her to greater speed. She felt strong and rested. So far, she had no pain in her foot, but she knew that she had not yet really put any strain on it.

The pony began to bring herself into the zone of concentration she needed to run a good race. It was hard with so many distractions. She tried to keep her mind off of her foot and the raucous crowd. Her driver had her up to a good pace now and she raised and lowered her knees, loosening and warming the muscles in her strong, lean thighs. The harness pulled against her front as she dragged the cart behind her. The new slave girl had learned quickly and she had adorned her with it correctly, making sure that the traces that led back to the sulky cart would be taut when she was in her running position. She was connected to the cart at five points. Two led from her harness at her shoulders and one from the middle of her back. The other two came from the shafts affixed to the waist belt. They all had to be in perfect unison for her to be able to apply maximum effort.

After about five minutes of running, Lightning felt her body warming. Her mind was becoming attuned to the timing of her strides. Her heart was starting to beat forcefully and her breathing was becoming deep and full. She passed the length of track which ran directly in front of the appreciative crowd. She had begun to tune them out. By the time she started the race, they would be just a faint noise.

She passed the gate that led from the paddock area, completing one lap of the 1500 meter track. She knew that her driver would run her through one more lap at a medium speed and then she would be ready.

As Lightning came around the home turn again, she noticed that the ache in her foot had increased slightly from her modest exertions. She was used to pain. She would wrap her mind around it and use it as a tool to spark her efforts. The other pony would be fast. That was for certain. This was not like one of the regular season meets where she might be put up against a pony who had been drafted just to fill in the other estate's racing card. No, this pony would be an expert runner, having defeated all the other expert runners she had faced in the tournament so far. Lightning would need to be able to draw deeply on her reserves of strength and endurance in order to win.

Up in the stands, Jake and Irkut watched Lightning's warm up with more than academic interest. She needed to win for the match race between her and Chocolate to be held the next day.

"Do you see?" Irkut asked Jake as he peered through his binoculars. "She's got a slight limp in her right leg. It's that foot injury."

Jake had been watching intently, but the limp had escaped his notice. Irkut was an expert while he was a novice and if the slender, medium build, ponygirl expert said there was a limp, then there was a limp. He hoped to hell that it did not slow her down.

Drabik was watching the tall, auburn tailed pony just as closely from up in the owner's clubhouse. He too saw the limp and he cursed his boss, Axmail Grobgy, for not canceling the race. On the other hand, if it was enough to cause her to lose the race and make the match race in which he might lose her forever be scratched, then it was worth risking a more permanent injury.

Drabik had his new, Italian slave girl kneeling next to his chair. Her hair had been shortened, giving her an interesting, modern look. He had rogered her royally last night and given her some more lashes just to keep her on her toes. She fucked him passionately afterwards. Now, he had her hands bound behind her and a long, thick gag in her mouth. She had taken his edge off a little while ago with her plump lips and her agile tongue. He had decided that she had been a good bargain.

Down on the track, the ponies were finishing their last warm up laps and were being maneuvered to the start line. Lightning had the outside rail as the higher seed. In a long race like the 3000 meter sulky, having the inside rail was not as much an advantage as in the shorter 1500 meter races, and so placement was of little concern. Lightning felt ready to go. Everything felt just as it should be. She placed her lead boot on the start line and dug it into the dirt for a good push off. All that was needed now was the signal to start.

The crowd hushed as the starting official raised the pistol into the air. Jerzi, her dwarfish driver, tightened his grip on the reins. There was a long pause during which over 9,000 pairs of ears and eyes waited for the shot to go off. And then, 'Bang!' the race began.

Lightning was poised to react immediately to the snap of her reins that signaled her to go. All of her weight was on her front leg. She was moving forward before the sharp snap of her reins echoed back down to her driver's hands. She got a good jump, but the other pony did too. Within seconds, she was driving herself to get up to speed. By the time ten or so strides had gone past, she was up to a running pace.

Lightning was a great finisher. As long as she kept herself within a length of the other pony, she had a decent shot at winning the race. She huffed and she puffed as her driver kept her just a half a length back from the other pony. She tried to drive the other pony out of her mind and just concentrate on the task of running. One leg in front of the other, knees raised high for maximum strides, her breathing deep and regulated, her heart beginning to pound.

At the ¾ pole of the first lap, Gypsy began to pull ahead. Lightning felt a tug on her reins accompanied by the snap of her driver's whip just over her shoulder and she increased her pace. The pain in her foot was becoming more pronounced. She tried to ignore it as she pounded her boots into the track.

Irkut had his glasses trained on the blue and green hooded pony. "It looks like Gypsy is making her move," she told Jake and the others.

"Let me see! Let me see!" Tanya exclaimed as she reached for Jake's binoculars.

"What does it mean?" Jake asked.

"It means that she's going to run Lightning down. Gypsy's had three years experience running this race and she has built up her endurance. If she can get a good pace going and keep it up for the entire next lap, then Lightning might be finished. She's got to hold herself within a length or a length and a half to stay in the race."

"Oh!" Tanya exclaimed. "She's falling behind!"

Sure enough, Lightning was now a full two lengths behind the stronger, more experienced pony. The ponygirl saw the other pony ahead of her and she yearned to increase her speed to stay close. But her driver was holding her back. It was his strategy that would be followed, not hers. She tried to put the view of the other pony's hindquarters out of her mind and concentrate on running.

When the ponies passed the ¼ pole in the second lap, Lightning was almost 3 lengths behind. It looked like the famous American ponygirl would not repeat her championship of the spring. If she did not, debate would rage during the off season as to whether Grobgy had been wise to shift her from the 1500 meter to the longer race or whether it was just because of her injury that she had failed.

Jerzi's racing strategy would be dissected and the strategy of the other driver applauded. But the race was not over yet. There was still ¾ of a lap to go.

Anton Drabik was ecstatic. He hated to do it, but he was rooting against Lightning and for the black tailed Gypsy. If Lightning lost, there would be no match race. He would be reunited with her as soon as the tournament was over. Once he had made his move and took over Grobgy's organization, she would belong to him. What would happen after that, he hadn't thought out yet. But having her was the first step to any future together.

Then, at the ½ pole, the whole race changed. Jerzi gave the ponygirl the signal to let it all out, to go at her maximum speed. Lightning pushed down hard on her right leg to increase her pace. As she did, she felt the wound in her foot open up. She grimaced, as much as a ponygirl could grimace with the lip stretching bit in her mouth, each time her right foot became planted on the ground. But rather than slowing her down, the painful sensations seemed to speed her up. Her whole being was focused on digging that right foot as deep as she could in the track for maximum leverage. The pain became a symbol of her bestial existence, something that had to be overcome. She knew that if she lost the race, she would go back to being just another ponygirl. She didn't want that. If she had to be an animal, to live her life silent and obedient, she wanted the comfort of knowing that she was special and not just another anonymous beast.

"Look!" Irkut exclaimed. "She's speeding up! She's making her move!"

Jake and the other occupants of the box, as well as about 9,000 other fans, stood to get a better look. The gap was decreasing steadily between Lightning and the black tailed pony. By the time they got to the ¾ pole, the gap between them had been reduced to 1 ½ lengths. Lightning was still in the race.

Drabik stood as well and cursed fate, cursed Jerzi, cursed Axmail Grobgy, his boss. The slave girl at his feet gave a shudder of fear. There were shouts and yells all through the owner's clubhouse encouraging the respective favorites. Grobgy, who was on the other side of the clubhouse from his hireling, gripped the arms of his chair as his pony rounded the home turn. "Come on Lightning! Come on Lightning! Come on Lightning!" he called out. Anya was there too. She urged the pony on with a mantra of her own. She too wanted her to win. She wanted the match race to go off. Then Lightning could fail and be gone from their estate forever, leaving Drabik to her and her alone. "Go Lightning! Go!" she yelled.

Lightning's mind was bursting with need, with determination, with courage. She had converted the pain in her foot from a liability to an asset. She wanted the pain, needed the pain to drive her on harder and harder. She grunted and groaned at each step. As she neared the other pony, she could hear the sounds of her ultimate efforts as well. As long as those sounds were ahead of her, Lightning would push her self harder and harder with each stride.

When the two ponies came out of the home turn, Lightning had advanced herself just past the wheels of the other sulky cart. Each step bought her another six inches or more of distance towards taking the lead. She felt the crack of her driver's whip on her shoulder and heard him screaming behind her. "Faster! Faster! Faster!" she yelled in her mind. She could see the finish line up ahead. "Arrrgh! Arrrgh! Arrrgh! Arrrgh!" she yelled as she strained for breath and dug deeply within herself for just one more ounce of strength.

At 250 meters, she was just behind the other pony's feet. At 200 she was at her hip. At 150, she was at her shoulder. At 100, they were neck and neck. It was anybody's race.

Jake was yelling and screaming with the rest of the crowd. He had never wanted anything that he had no control over so much in his life. He was self reliant, bet only on sure things, took care of every detail. But there was nothing he could do to help Lightning win the race. His palms were sweaty and his heart pounded in his chest. "Come on Lightning!" he yelled.

Lightning's uncle, Michael Burnham, was urging her on too. He wanted possession of his beautiful, fast, strong niece so much he could taste it. His feelings were anything but avuncular. He wanted to possess her, own her, feel her lips circumnavigating his prick. And when he wanted something, he almost always got it.

The object of his lusts was still pounding away at the track. Gypsy, her opponent, had not gotten to where she was without having heart and desire as well. She was pumping her legs furiously, struggling desperately to regain the lead. At 50 meters the ponies were still shoulder to shoulder. Dirt flew up in chunks as they pierced the track with their sturdy boots.

Lightning was at the end of her reserves. She had almost nothing left to give. Her mind, for an instant, focused on the prospects of losing, of being an also ran, of being dropped back into the pony herd. It was all she needed. Her pained right foot dug deeply into the turf and her knee bent and she gave her body a mighty push. She reached her leg out as far as it could go and repeated the effort with her left boot. For seven agonizing steps, she poured her whole being into her efforts. It was just enough. She crossed the finish line leading the unfortunate Gypsy by a little more than three inches. Victory!

CHAPTER TWO

It took the gasping pony ten strides to slow herself down back into a trot. She knew she had won and her mind and body exalted. She heard her name being chanted by the crowd, "*Molnya! Molnya! Molnya!*" Her driver led her once more around the track in her victory lap and then to the winner's circle where her owner, trainer and various hangers on awaited. One of them was Anya. She made sure that she nestled up against Drabik when the obligatory photo was taken. In the print on the wall of the Tournament Clubhouse, it looks, at first, like an optical illusion, but, in fact, Anya's hand had laid hold of Drabik's thigh as the picture was snapped. Of course, no one saw that until much later.

Lightning was driven back to her campsite, a thick, colorful garland around her neck. The other drivers and grooms shouted out their congratulations to Jerzi as they went, which he acknowledged with a tip of his cap. The exalted pony fully expected that she would be granted the boon of a long, passionate bout with her driver and maybe others. She was surprised and filled with disappointment when she was not.

While every person at the tournament knew that Lightning had one more race to run before she could truly celebrate, she, of course, did not. Not until her driver hopped down from the sulky cart and then, after ordering her to her knees while still encased in her harness, he held his hand in front of her face with a single digit pointed upwards. "One," he intoned in English. At the spring tournament, just before the race that first made her a ponygirl champion, the diminutive man had made the same gesture, indicating to Lightning that she had one more race to run. She understood its meaning now, but not its import. Why would she have another race to run? Hadn't she just won the championship of her division? What could it mean?

The distraught pony had little time to contemplate her future. Jerzi removed the bit from her mouth and then drew his fleshy sword from his racing pants. He quickly brought it to erection with his hand and then jerked and stroked it until his face had turned red and his breath had become heavy. Lightning knew what was expected of her. She opened her mouth dutifully to receive her master's spunk. It was a sure sign that there would be no orgasm for her tonight. She would have to endure another night of agonized frustration as the slave girl drove her again and again near to the edge of satisfaction. There was still one more race to run and she would have to earn her pleasure.

Jerzi was huffing and puffing now with the exertions of yanking his tool. He groaned and his spunk began to spurt from his wand and splash into the gaping mouth of the ponygirl. The acrid, semi-sweet taste would stay with her until her dinner time, a reminder her of what she was, as if that was necessary.

When finished, and after letting the last drop of his cum drip onto the ponygirl's lips, Jerzi reinstalled her bit and closed himself up. The black haired slave girl, Amanda, had been left bound and gagged while he was at the track and he released her now so that she could complete her tasks of caring for the valuable ponygirl champion. Amanda jumped to her duties. She took hold of the ring in Lightning's nose and led her to the rub down table at the edge of the clearing. She lay her down across it after removing her harness and began a skilled manipulation of the ponygirl's muscles to prevent any cramping. Amanda had heard some of the other slave girls talking about the projected match race between the two American ponies. She had no idea what it really meant, but she was afraid that it might mean that she would lose the right to take care of the fit, muscular, former woman.

She had grown to like her new job. The feel of the pony's hard flesh beneath her hands contrasted with her fluffy, ample, soft breasts and the flesh between her thighs. Lightning was on her belly now, her arms attached to the top of the inclined table so that the slave girl could get at her entire back. Once she was turned over, and Amanda began to work on the fronts of her thighs, the slave girl would sample the pony's delights by suckling at her breasts and caressing the folds of her sex until the racing animal was panting and shuddering with need. Amanda yearned to make her come. She enjoyed seeing the fearsome, powerful female erupt into convulsions of pleasure. But for that she would have to wait. There was one more race to run.

Drabik worked his way to Jerzi's camp site. The camping grounds were filled with celebrating champion jockeys and trainers as well as the more numerous unsuccessful ones. Except for the occasional spoil sport, the drivers and their helpers, being a tightly knit group, usually shared willingly in the celebrations of their confreres. Vodka was spilled by the gallon full and many a ponygirl was amply rewarded for her hard work while kneeling in the soft grass or on the dry, dusty earth. Drabik forwent the many offers of salutations and ponygirl flesh. He was on a mission. Today meant nothing to him. Tomorrow was all.

When he entered Jerzi's campsite, the diminutive driver was seated on his suitably sized camp chair easing back a glassful of vodka. The dwarfish driver was exhausted from the exertions of the championship race and the not inconsiderable stress of needing to win. After all, it was his negligence that allowed Lightning to suffer her injuries to begin with. For him, too, there was one more race to run. Jerzi's face darkened when he saw the scar faced killer and ponygirl trainer enter his camp. Just when he had started to relax, his tension was instantly renewed.

"Congratulations, Jerzi," Drabik spat out. "You get to live one more day."

"Now, Anton," the small man intoned, "there's no reason to talk like that. She's won the championship. I've done everything I could."

"The championship means nothing to me," Drabik answered. "It would have been far better if you had lost as far as I'm concerned. If you lose the race tomorrow and Lightning is claimed by that bastard American, you'll wish that you had never been born."

Sweat started to roll down Jerzi's distorted face. A pit opened up in his belly. Drabik's reputation as a cruel, psychotic killer was well earned. And he knew that the dark visaged man was not prone to exaggeration.

"She should win easily, Anton," Jerzi protested. "After all, *Shokoladniy's* never run the 3000 meter race. And she's injured to boot! I think the American has lost his mind."

"I don't trust him," Drabik shot back. "He wouldn't have challenged *Molnya* unless he was sure that he had a good chance to win. Who would risk losing a champion pony like that on a whim? He's got something up his sleeve all right. I wouldn't be surprised to learn that he's been practicing the pony for the 3000 all along."

"It won't help him," Jerzi answered. The hand holding his glass of vodka was trembling slightly. Rather than spill it, he shot its contents back into his throat. After taking a moment to relish the liquor's fiery descent, he added, "*Molnya's* the best. I've never seen a pony like her."

"Yes, Jerzi, that's true. But she's injured too, remember? It's going to be a matter of which pony is injured worse, something we wouldn't have to worry about if it weren't for your stupidity."

Drabik's eyes were on the kneeling form of the curvaceous, desirable creature he had just mentioned. Amanda had restored the pony's gag to her mouth and had led her to the large, thick mounting post in the middle of the encampment. Her nose ring was connected to the post by a chain long enough to allow her to kneel in the dirt, her thighs spread widely, her hairless slit beckoning to the impassioned ponygirl trainer. He watched her heavy, lust inspiring breasts sway slightly as she held herself erect to meet his gaze. Her tattooed belly undulated as she breathed, making the yellow, rampant wolf etched there seemingly come alive. Her upper chest was emblazoned in two inch high, bright blue, Cyrillic letters with the name he had given her, *Molnya*. All of him wanted no more than to dash across the thirty or so feet that separated them and press his body against her naked flesh. "Soon!' he thought. "Soon.".

Lightning did not speak Russian, but she knew that the men's' argument was about her. Her foot ached, but she was still filled with the exaltation of her victory. What this additional race was all about, she had not a clue. It seemed very important to the men. She was starting to have a bad feeling about it, as if the race was much more than just a race. But what could it mean?

She returned her lover's gaze. Her eyes were masked by her soft, head encompassing, blue hood. Her racing hood had been removed and she was wearing her everyday, solid blue one. So while she could detect the need and worry in the man's eyes, her face was an apparent mask of indifference. She could communicate only with her body and she arched her back to better present her naked pulchritude to her master. She yearned for his lips upon them, to feel his hard, scarred hands caressing her flesh, to have his cock slide between her thighs and take possession of her. Racing season was over. For better or worse, she would soon be returned to the ponybarn back at the estate. There she would face whatever torments her trainer's black haired lover would inflict on her. Knowing that her trainer's lust would be waiting for her there as well made any pain or humiliation she would suffer at the cruel woman's hands pale.

Drabik made a decision, one that went against everything he knew about ponygirl training, against all protocols of ponygirl racing.

"Go have a drink somewhere, Jerzi," he said curtly. "I want to be alone with the pony."

"Now, Anton, you know that…"

"Get out of here!" Drabik roared. "Don't forget, if you were dead there would be no claiming race tomorrow! I can easily arrange it!"

Jerzi meekly rose from his tiny chair and drifted out of the campsite. He gave one last look over his shoulder before disappearing down the service trail.

Drabik watched the dwarf disappear. Once he was out of sight, he turned to the black haired slave girl who was kneeling near Jerzi's little chair. She was trembling with fear. She didn't understand a word of Russian, but she was sure the dispute was over the ponygirl. She hoped like hell that she hadn't done anything wrong. She knew what had happened to the last slave girl who fucked with Lightning.

"Go get your slave hood!" Drabik spat out at the full breasted, naked girl in English. She jumped to her feet and ran inside Jerzi's trailer. She came out with the leather hood within moments and, kneeling before the terror inducing master, proffered it to him.

The slave hood went on easily, the attached gag filling the slave girl's mouth and the blinding hood pulled over her face. Once Drabik had the ear plugs situated in her aural canals, he strapped the hood tightly closed. The slave girl could neither see nor hear what went on around her. Grabbing her soft shoulder, he spun her around and locked her wrists behind her. He then callously shoved her to the ground where he locked her ankle bracelets together.

Cut off totally from her environment, deprived of all means of mobility, Amanda prepared herself for a long wait in darkened solitude.

Satisfied that the slave girl would have nothing to report to her sister slaves, a grapevine as dependable as Western Union, Drabik turned himself to the object of his lust and his obsession. Lightning had watched her lover, her true master, send the slave girl into total isolation. She set herself tall on her knees in anticipation of her trainer's approach, for she knew that he intended to embrace her. All of her body yearned for him, strained for his touch. She prepared herself for the joy of finally feeling his hands on her after so long.

Drabik lowered himself to his knees before the ponygirl. He too was afire with need. He ran his hands over her soft shoulders, down her upper portion of her imprisoned arms and then along her torso to her hips. "At long last," he thought. "Why does my body and mind burn for her so?"

The killer and ponygirl trainer brought his hands up slowly until the pony's large, malleable breasts were in them. He felt the pony lean forward to fill his hands with her large mounds. Her nipples were hardened nubbins in anticipation of her use. Her body smelled of sweat and arousal.

The killer squeezed the hefty, firm orbs tightly. His passion rose as he luxuriated in the sensation of her hot skin, her pleasantly soft, yet firm breasts. He heard the pony moan, the closest thing to speech that a ponygirl was permitted.

"I've missed you, little *Molnya*," he said to her in Russian, his voice heavy with his desire. He leaned over and took first one thick teat and then the other into his mouth, giving them both a long, hard suckle. They tasted of the salt of the pony's sweat, her exertions. He felt the pony's body press into him, her knees spread just a little wider, heard her moans growing deeper.

He raised his head from his enjoyment of the pony's breasts and let his hands drift down her pale, round hips and then along the outside of her thick, strong thighs. Eight, almost nine months of constant running, usually pulling a heavy cart behind her, had made her legs as strong as any man's, stronger. The salve that was applied to her body every day had kept her body soft and as white as alabaster in spite of her continual exposure to the strong, Kalikastani summer sun.

Drabik yearned to strip himself nude and ravish the ponygirl right there in the dust. But he didn't have time for that. Jerzi would soon be back. It was imperative that he communicate with the desirable beast. Although he had not spoken a word in English to her for all the many days that he had known her, he needed to make her understand what was at stake.

As his right hand captured the pony's dilated, moisture laden slit, Drabik leaned over and whispered in her ear.

"Soon you will be mine, little ponygirl. No one will be able to separate us, no one! My flesh burns for you. When I own you totally, I'll fuck you every day and let you suckle my hot cock morning, noon and night. Would you like that, ponygirl? Do you desire me too?"

Lightning, through her impassioned haze, was shocked at the familiar sounds of English in her ear. It took a moment to register that the man was actually speaking to her. As the man's meaning became clear, joy burst through her muscular frame. Did she desire him? She desired nothing else!

The happy pony made a mewing sound of approval through her mouth filling gag. The hand that was tormenting her flush crevasse was driving her rapidly towards completion. Oh, how wonderful it felt to be in her master's hands again! She knew that this was the very man who had stolen her humanity away, had forced her to accept her reduction to a mute animal, driven her sexual needs to heights unimaginable to her before her dehumanization, made her accepting of all the cocks and tongues and hands that had violated her, the man who had whipped her many times so cruelly that she thought that she would die. She knew that she should hate him, but she had come to accept her new life as a ponygirl. All hope of rescue or escape had long ago been driven from her. Her former life was a mere shadow of a memory, something that occasionally cropped up in her restless dreams. This was her reality now. The hand that was caressing her lubricated, excited folds was her reality. She was a faceless, voiceless creature that existed only to please her masters, and the man who was caressing her, whispering in her ear for the first time in a way that she could actually understand his words, was the master she longed to serve.

Drabik sensed the pony's expression of the mutuality of their lust. Her shrouded, anonymous head was leaning on his shoulder. Her breath was coming heavy. His fingers penetrated deeply inside her as her drove her lusts on and on. He spoke again to her, sure that she would hear him through her excitement.

"There's only one thing that can keep us apart. The man who owns you now has committed you to a claiming race tomorrow. You will be racing against the pony that won the 1500 meter championship. If you lose, the other pony's owner will take possession and ownership of you. Tomorrow, you must run harder than you ever have run before. If you lose, we will be separated forever. You must win! You must!"

The agitated pony heard the man's words and understood their import even through her sexual delirium. "No! No!" she thought. "I will not lose! I can't! I couldn't bear the thought of being all alone again! I must win!"

Suddenly, the efforts of her master's expert caresses to her lush sex bore fruit. Her pussy contracted hard as her orgasm began. "Mmmmmmmmmm! Mmmmmmmmmmm!" she moaned. "Oh yes! Oh yes! Oh yes!" she thought as her whole body received the waves of pleasure that issued forth from her delirious slit. "Oh, God! I need this man! I need him! Please, God, don't let it happen!" Each contraction of her womb sent a spasm of pleasure through her. "This is the way it will be," she thought. "This is what I want. If I must be a ponygirl, let me belong to him!" She groaned again, her whole body shaking as the pulses of pleasure from her sex poured through her and then, finally faded into a warm, luxurious aftermath.

As the shuddering of her body eased, Drabik slowed his attentions to her quim. Her breasts were pressed up hard against him. Her chest was heaving as she struggled to regain her breath. His free hand was lying across her strong back, absorbing her heat. Her long, auburn ponytail, sprouting from the sea of blue that was her head, fluttered back and forth as she recovered her sensibilities.

"I'm going to leave you now, little ponygirl," he told her. "I'll be watching you tomorrow. Run the race of your life and you will soon belong to me!"

Lightning watched, with regret, her master's strong, wide back as he walked away until he left her sight. She didn't know whether to exult with joy or tremble from fear. She was going to belong to him! That was what he said. She didn't know the full import of what it meant, but she did know that it meant, at least, that they would be together. She thought of the discs dangling between her silken thighs, suspended from her labia. She had seen them only briefly when shown herself in the mirror, but she knew that it carried the name and emblem of her owner. Soon, she would have her true master's emblem there, proclaiming her as his and his alone. She pressed her thighs together in anticipation.

But would she? If she lost the race tomorrow, they would be separated forever! It was so unfair! After all she had gone through, all she had suffered, just when something was going to happen to ameliorate her plight, she was faced with the possibility of losing everything.

Although she didn't belong to her trainer, she at least had enjoyed contact with him, even though that brought with it the wrath of his apparent girlfriend, the tall, black haired, young woman. If she lost the race, though, she would be worse off than before. Who would care for her at the estate of her prospective new owner? Who would love her as her trainer did? Her conversion to an animal would be complete, with no one to relish the spark of humanity that she still kept inside in spite of everything that they had done to her. She had to win tomorrow! She just had to!

It was about twenty minutes later that Jerzi came strolling back. When he entered he campsite, he saw his slave girl all trussed up like a roast at the market. The ponygirl was where he had left her. Why did Drabik want to be alone with her, he thought to himself. What did he do? Jerzi saw that Amanda was wearing her slave hood. Why did Drabik want no witnesses? He apparently didn't even want someone to hear him.

Was he talking to the ponygirl? That would be a terrible interference with his dominion over her as her driver during racing season, no to mention counterproductive to her training. Ponygirls needed to realize and accept that they weren't human any more. Talking to them did them a great disservice as it made it harder to work them as they needed to be worked. It gave them hope that they would be made human again, be treated like a woman, not an animal. A ponygirl who had even a shred of belief that she would be saved from her fate was inevitably resistant to full and complete obedience. Failure to please a trainer or a driver meant pain. The dashing of the pony's hopes of redemption, and they inevitably would be dashed, no ponygirl had ever escaped or been freed, would recreate the despair of her early days as a pony. So talking to a ponygirl exposed her only to misery and unhappiness.

Lightning, of course, showed no emotion on her face, but Jerzi was an expert at assaying a ponygirl's moods. She looked to him just a little distant. Her shoulders were rounded and her back seemed to sag just a bit. Her head was held at what appeared to be a thoughtful, concerned angle. Ponygirls weren't supposed to think. There was only one remedy for that.

The small man ignored the trussed up body of the black haired slave girl and retrieved the long, thick riding crop that he kept on a nail next to the door to his trailer. He turned and strode purposely over to where the ponygirl knelt affixed to the tall, round, heavy pole.

Lightning saw the whip in her driver's hand. She knew what it meant. Somehow, her driver knew that something had transpired between her and her trainer and she was to be punished for it. A sea of resentment and anger welled up in her. It wasn't her fault! She had no choice in what was done with her!

Jerzi stood for a moment before the kneeling ponygirl, making sure that he had her full attention. He waited for a moment, letting the imminence of her punishment sink in. The pony needed to know who was boss. For now, it was him, not that bastard Drabik.

Staring back at her driver, who stood no taller than she did when she was kneeling, she realized that he was right. She needed to be punished. She needed to have all her focus on what she was and what she had to do. Even a moment's hesitancy in obeying her driver could cost her the race. It wasn't that she wanted to be punished. Her body was trembling, as it always did, at the sight of a whip in one of the masters' hands. She knew that the pain would be agonizing. She also knew that she needed to put all thoughts of her future out of her mind. A good whipping would help her remember what she was and what, for all intents and purposes, she would remain forever.

The dwarfish driver's arms were as strong as any man's. When he reared back and delivered a resounding stroke of the crop across the pony's luscious breasts, it made a loud slapping sound and was followed almost immediately by a deep, mournful groan from the pony. A long line of red sprung up immediately where the crop had kissed her flesh. The pony shuffled on its knees, grinding them in the dust in an attempt to assuage the intense pain he had delivered to it and to crush any thoughts of trying to avoid her desserts. When a pony was whipped, she was trained to stand and take it. Flinching or turning away only exacerbated the punishment. It took them a long time to build up the discipline to absorb the blows of a whip without shying away in panic. The whip was a good teacher, though, and they learned their duties soon enough.

"Crack!" The second blow landed across Lightning's breasts. "Ummmmmmmmmmmmmmm!" she moaned un-happily. To Lightning, it was as if someone had taken a knife and drawn it across them. The pain lingered long after the blow had been delivered. "Ohhhhhhhhh! Ohhhhhhhh!" she tried to say. But her mouth was, of course, stilled, and all that emerged was another moan.

Five times Jerzi laid the riding crop across the miserable pony's flesh. Her hooded head swayed back and forth between blows and her moans were a constant, deep, anguished humming as they emerged from behind her gag,

When he was done, he was sweating heavily. Nothing drove his lusts more than whipping a female, be she human or pony. He could use the ponygirl's mouth, but he felt the need to sink his cock deep inside a sea of flesh. There would be no fucking for the pony until she had won the race tomorrow. He turned his head and saw the slave girl lying in the dirt. Her full breasts were squashed beneath her and her hands wriggled nervously behind her, bound together by her wrist cuffs. Her naked, beauteous behind was twitching invitingly.

Jerzi tossed the whip aside and, as he stepped quickly to where the slave girl lay in the dirt, he lowered his fly and fished his man sized cock from its lair. When he reached her, he didn't hesitate. There was no time to loosen her legs and get at her delightful pussy. He would fuck her in the ass just as she was. The fact that her legs were bound together would make the dainty hole just that more tight around his cock.

Amanda was startled when she felt the ponygirl driver's hands take hold of her rear globes. She had no idea that he had come back. She knew it was him instantly. He had a touch that sent thrills through her. She felt him vault one leg over her conjoined thighs and his hands separate her rear cheeks. When she felt his hard prick press against the gates to her bowels, a wave of lust passed through her. She had never liked ass fucking before, but with the little man, as she thought of him, it was different. He had a magic cock that sent her into delirium whenever it entered her.

The prone slave girl felt the rigid, thick instrument squeeze inside her rear aperture. The entrance was dry and made all the tighter by her posture. She felt pain as the membranes were stretched and abraded by the dwarf's fat cock. After a moment, though, her lust took command and she willed her bung hole to loosen and accept the little man's worship of it.

Jerzi moaned as his cock slowly sank to its hilt inside the hot portal. This English girl was good, he thought. But then, wasn't ass fucking an English sport?

It only took a few thrusts until the dwarf's cock was running easily back and forth in the bound slave girl's rear. Jerzi supported himself with his gnarled hands on the slave girl's back as he sawed his pleasure within her. His knees rode up against her thighs. The slave girl was wriggling and moaning as he assaulted her. "What a lustful bitch," he thought. When the season was over, and the race was won tomorrow, he would demand to be allowed to keep her. His mind reeled with the thoughts of a long winter of pleasure with her. And she took a whip well too!

Feeling his cock's explosion begin to build, Jerzi increased the pace of his thrusts. He growled and grunted as the pleasurable sensations coursed through him. It built and built and built and built. If he wanted, he could fuck the slave girl for an hour without coming. But not today. Now he needed release. He felt the door open and then his body's massive, built up energy released itself through the tiny hole at the end of his rigid rod.

"Arrrrgh! Arrrrrrgh!" he shouted as he came. His eyes rolled back and his body sagged.

Amanda felt the cock pulsing against the ring of her anus. "Oh god! Oh god! Oh god!" she thought as her pussy began to convulse in reciprocal delight. "Mmmmmmmmm! Mmmmmmmmmm! Mmmmmmmmmmm!" she moaned through her gag. She strained at her bonds as her whole body shook. Amanda had had many masters since she had been kidnapped almost two years ago. But the little man was, in her opinion, the best! What he did to her with his cock!"

Lightning watched the two human beings rut in the dirt. Her breasts still pulsed with pain from her beating, but her pussy yearned for fulfillment nonetheless. She hadn't been fucked for days, an agonizing state for a ponygirl, whose life was built around sexual enjoyment. "Soon" she thought. "Soon." After tomorrow's race she would be fucked like a hound dog in heat. And then, her master would claim her. She just had to win! She just had to!

CHAPTER THREE

Jake, Tanya and Irkut had stopped by one of the crowded, noisy refreshment tents after Chocolate's and Lightning's championship runs. Irkut led them, the pint sized man elbowing his way through the throng, to a just vacated table. They were all in a celebratory mood. The tent was served by a crew of delectable slave girls, all scurrying around delivering huge steins of ale. Jake watched admiringly as a nude, busty blond, her golden colored hair done back in woven braids, delivered eight, heavy, glass steins, four in each hand, to a table of inebriated guests, rough looking men, all dressed in shoddy workmen's clothes. Her heavy breasts swayed out from her lithe body invitingly as she stooped to place the steins on the table. One of the men circled her waist with his arm and pulled her to his lap.

"How about a little kiss, Ingrid?" he asked her lasciviously. "Give me one of those luscious tits and let me smother my face in it!"

Obediently, the girl arched her back and let the man encompass her thick nipple in his mouth. His free hand was running up between her shapely legs. "Mmmmmm-mmmm!" he moaned as he subsumed her breast between his lips up past her areola.

The other men were shouting out drunken encouragements. Ingrid's arm was around her assailant's broad neck and Jake watched as her face recorded the attentions to her melon sized mound. When the man emerged from her teat, he was smiling. "How much, *suka*?" he asked her. He wasn't asking the price of the beer.

"Thirty zlotskis," the girl replied. Her breathing had become heavy and Jake saw a tell tale blush of arousal on her chest. It surrounded and accentuated the blue, Cyrillic writing tattooed there denoting her name. The girl was undoubtedly of German origin both from her name and the harsh, guttural accent of her voice. She either knew English, the lingua franca of slave girls, before being shanghaied to Kalikastan or she learned it at the point of a whip since her arrival. Nobody spoke to slave girls in Russian or Kalikastani, other than a few words of command. Keeping them ignorant of those languages helped keep them subservient.

"Cheap at twice the price!" the man exclaimed. He looked at his confreres with a broad grin. "I'll be back in a while," he announced. "Who wants seconds?"

His companions all clamored for the right to follow him in partaking of the beautiful girl's flesh. "Don't mark her all up, Bruda!" one of the other men shouted out.

Bruda had risen to his feet and, after locking the slave girl's hands behind her by her wrist bracelets, spun her around and took hold of the ring in her slave collar.

"How much for a whipping, slut," he asked. Jake saw a splash of panic cross the girl's face.

"F,fifty zlotkis, master," she replied tremulously.

"A bargain!" Bruda replied heartily. He turned to his friends. "I may be a little longer than I thought. This cunt's breasts look like they were made for the whip! You can let me know your opinions when I bring her back!"

All the other men laughed. Bruda dragged the sorrowful girl behind him as he walked to the back of the tent. There was a row of smaller tents behind it all appointed with cots for fucking the serving girls and a ring dangling from their centers to attach their wrists to so that they could be properly beaten.

Jake felt a pang of sorrow for the unfortunate girl. On the other hand, the thought of delving between her pale, silken thighs had been appealing to him.

"Don't get any ideas, Jake," Tanya said, laughing. "You need to save yourself up for me tonight. And don't worry, I'm sure we'll use all your man cream up."

Irkut joined Tanya in her laughter. Tanya was wearing a loose, sapphire blue, satin blouse that buttoned just below the joining of her sumptuous breasts. Her loose mounds pushed invitingly against the smooth fabric. Her skirt was a deep, blue denim and hung loose just below her knees. Jake knew that there was nothing on underneath it since he had slipped his hand up there while they were kissing earlier. He unconsciously brought his hand to his nose and inhaled the scent of her arousal.

A dark haired brunette brought them three steins of ale. The drinks were free. The owner made his money on his slave girls' pussies. Give a man a few servings of the heavy, tart ale native to these parts and the sight of a beautiful, available, naked slave girl, and he and his money would be soon parted.

Irkut lifted his stein. It was topped off with a three inch layer of thick, white foam. The brew was dark, almost black. Jake guessed that it was probably about 20 proof.

"Here's to success!" Irkut announced. He was the one who had whipped, literally, Chocolate into her tip top racing form. He had broken her to her bit, as the saying went. He was undoubtedly due a large bonus.

"Success!" all three of them shouted as they clanged their heavy steins together. There was about 16 ounces of ale in each one.

The trio put the steins to their lips and began inhaling the potent brew. In the spirit of their celebration, they chugged the hearty ale down until the three steins were empty. Irkut finished first and he slammed his mug down on the coarse, wooden table. Jake was next. His brain was swirling and he felt his belly bloating.

Tanya was still hard at work. Her head was poised back and the liquid was flowing in a steady stream down her gullet.

"*Gratchya! Gratchya! Gratchya! Gratchya!*" Irkut called out rhythmically, slamming his stein down on the table at each exclamation. Jake, although he didn't know the meaning of the Kalikastani word, joined in.

"*Gratchya! Gratchya! Gratchya!*" the pair of men called out in encouragement to the slender but voluptuous girl.

Finally, Tanya slammed her stein down on the table, grinning from ear to ear. "*Gratchya!*" she exclaimed back at the men. They all laughed.

Irkut turned and signaled for another round.

"What the fuck does '*gratchya*' mean?" Jake asked his lover. She was still recovering her breath. Ale had dripped down her chest and her breasts were enticingly outlined as the wet fabric clung to them.

Tanya grinned. Her face was flush from her endeavors. Her plump lips made Jake's little boy rise as he thought of how they would be encircling his cock later.

"There's no word for it in English," Tanya answered him. "It's a cross between 'fuck you' and 'hooray'. It depends on the context. When a Kalikastani smashes his finger with a hammer, he yells '*Gratchya!*' When the ponygirl he's bet on finishes the race first, he yells, '*Gratchya!*' When his girlfriend takes his cock in her mouth, he moans 'Oh, *gratchya!*'"

"I'll have to remember that for later," Jake said, smiling.

"You better," Tanya spat back. Another round of ale was delivered by a short, naked, redheaded girl. Her hair was loose down to her diminutive shoulders. She had small, pointy breasts that jutted out deliciously, each one a little more than a mouthful.

The girl carted the empty steins away and the three friends began to work on the second round, more slowly this time.

"It's a miracle," Irkut said. "First of all, the chances of a yearling pony capturing a championship is almost impossible. No pony had done it until Lightning did it in the spring. Although she was clearly a pony with heart, I never thought Chocolate would do it when I started training her. And then her recovery from her injury that seemed to have put her out of the tournament for good. I'll have to send Dr. Kevsky a present after I get home. Maybe a nice little slave girl for her collection."

"She'll be busy with all the new ones she's gotten, thanks to Jake," Tanya said.

"Thanks to me?" Jake asked querulously.

"Yes, you," Tanya answered. "It was on your advice that she asked Mr. Burnham for that cute, little Malaysian girl, Orchid. He agreed right away and threw in the four fresh girls that he used in his party the other night for the entertainment of the guests. I can still see them circling above the stage, each receiving a bite from the cowboy's whip, and then flying off, each one screaming in panic. It was a marvelous show!"

The trio continued to pour down their ale as they reminisced about Burnham's extravaganza. The conversation, though, quickly steered itself back to Chocolate and her victory.

"She's such a fine pony, it will be a shame if we lose her tomorrow," Irkut opined.

"What did you say?" Jake asked, taken aback by what he thought he heard.

Irkut looked at him intently. "I said that it will be a shame if we lose her tomorrow."

"How can that be?" Jake asked, panic creeping into his voice.

"Well, it's a claiming race," Irkut replied. "I thought that you knew that. Winner takes all."

"That's not what Burnham told me!" Jake spat out, his ire rising. "He said he put up a share in the pipeline project against Lightning. Grobgy would stand to make millions."

"Millions, schmilllions," Irkut replied. "Grobgy wouldn't risk his prize pony for money."

"You mean that if Chocolate loses, she'll belong to Grobgy?"

"Of course," Irkut answered. "There'd be no other point to racing."

A vast chasm opened in Jake's belly. He had recruited Jackie, the brown skinned whore from Chicago, to become a ponygirl so that they could win Maddy back. He hadn't told her that her freedom would be at stake in the race. He had promised that he would get her out once the Maddy thing was settled one way or the other. If Grobgy won her, there would be no way he could ever save her. She'd remain a ponygirl for life!

The ale turned sour in Jake's belly. "I've got to go," he said almost vacantly.

"Where are you going, Jake?" Tanya asked, startled by her lover's reaction. Everybody knew what a claiming race was in Kalikastan, didn't they? Apparently, no one had told Jake. But why was he so concerned?

"She's just a ponygirl, Jake," Tanya told him. "Pony-girls come and go. It won't matter much to her whose barn she lives in. Her life will be more or less the same. Does she mean that much to you?"

Jake cast a quick look at Irkut. The dedicated ponygirl trainer had told him just a couple days ago that he would stop anyone who did anything to threaten the peculiar national sport of Kalikastan. Jake had a feeling that Irkut was pretty close to guessing what was going on. He didn't want him to get any closer to solving the puzzle.

"No, not at all," Jake answered. "Like you said, she's just a ponygirl. It's just that it would be a shame after all we did to make sure that she won the championship. And she's a delectable fuck."

"She's that all right," Irkut agreed. His sense that all was not right with the Americans, Burnham and Jake, had been heightened once again. It was as if the race tomorrow was more than a sporting event to them. He had to get to the bottom of it.

"I'm just going to go over to her camp and see that she's all right. She was limping pretty bad after her last race," Jake added.

"Now don't you think for one minute that I'm going to let you fuck her once more for old times sake, Jake," Tanya shot out. "Tonight, you belong to me!" It was as close to anger as Jake had ever seen her. It was almost as if she had grown claws right in front of him.

"Nothing like that, honest," Jake answered quickly. "I just want to see how she is. That's all. I made a promise to you and I always keep my promises."

Yeah, I always keep my promises, Jake thought. "What about my promise to Jackie?"

Jake tossed back the last of his ale, trying to act nonchalant. "I thought that you were going to go help your mother pack up," he asked the beautiful tigress.

"Yes, I am," Tanya answered. "And you better be there in less than a half hour or I'll come looking for you with a knife."

Jake believed that she would.

"I've got to check on Czarina," Irkut interjected. "And then I'm going to make a call at the milk pony tent and see my little strawberry girl."

Jake and Tanya looked at him and laughed. Irkut's enamoration with the daughter of the owner of the full breasted ponies who had been, so to speak, put out to pasture, was a source of humor to Jake and all of Tanya's family. The well endowed young girl was in milk herself. Irkut's statement of intent had broken the tension between the three. Jake had gone to the milk pony tent with Irkut two days ago and had the benefit of drawing sustenance from one of the ponies there, a delightful experience. It was another thing that he would miss about Kalikastan.

Irkut drained his stein and Tanya did the same. The three rose from their seats and for a moment, there was an awkward silence. Finally, Jake said. "I'll see you in a half an hour, Tanya. I promise. I wouldn't miss our night together for the world."

Tanya smiled. "It will be a night to remember, I promise," she said saucily.

The three went their separate ways. Czarina, the gargantuan pony once named Maureen, was at her trailer located in the southern portion of the ponygirl encampment. Chocolate's was more to the north.

"Have fun tonight," Jake told Irkut, waiving at him as he walked away.

As he made his way to the ponygirl encampment, Jake had anything but fun on his mind. Somehow, he had to let Chocolate know what really was at stake tomorrow. She deserved to know what would happen if she failed. One good thing, though: since she would know, she would surely pour her whole heart and soul into the race.

As he strode purposely to Chocolate's encampment, his thoughts turned to his perfidious boss. He had had a feeling for a long time that Burnham was not being totally honest with him. He had grown to believe that if he won Maddy back there was little chance that Jake would be allowed to take her out of the country.

Burnham had fallen lock, stock and barrel into the Kalikastani way of life. They were supposed to rescue Maddy and get out, but there was every sign that Burnham was intent on making Kalikastan his permanent home. He had started his own slave training facility. There were plans to build a casino and resort for jaded Western businessmen on Lake Novrograd. He had built up his stock of personal slave girls and ponygirls way beyond what was necessary for mere cover for their operations, and he had moved half of his corporate headquarters here. No, if he won Maddy, Maddy would remain Lightning for a long, long time, probably forever. And she was his own niece too!

Jake had plans to outfox the bastard and get Maddy out anyway. He never let go of a job once he started it, even if his 'employer' got cold feet. He had resigned himself to the fact that his effort to save Maddy would fail if Chocolate lost the race tomorrow, but he had never thought that he would not be able to free the lithesome, hardy brown skinned pony. Now he knew that if Chocolate lost the race, his mission would be a double failure.

As Jake strolled his way to Chocolate's encampment, he was being followed. Irkut had doubled back after parting ways and was trailing the American, determined to find out what Jake was up to.

When Jake arrived at the camp, about a dozen wellwishers, other trainers and drivers, were gathered around celebrating his victory. Chocolate was on her knees, her mouth engrossed in suckling the stiffened tool of her dwarfish driver, Giorgi, who was standing before her. Her thighs were spread for balance, her hands, of course, bound behind her, and she was bent over, leaning to address the dwarf's tool, making her torso almost perpendicular to the ground. The garland of colorful, late summer wildflowers with which she had been adorned when her owner received his trophy and she her golden championship disk for her collar, was still hanging around her neck.

The desirable, chocolate colored pony was working the dwarf's cock by jerking her head back and forth. With each jerk, her brown beauties jumped and swayed. She was lean and taut, just like all the other ponygirls. Her thighs looked as muscular as any wrestlers. Her head was covered by the black and gold colors of Burnham's estate; her ponytail was dancing and flurrying this way and that as a result of her endeavors. She was a sight to behold.

Jake remembered her lovely body well, having fucked her many times back in Chicago. He thought of their last time together there, the night he had put the proposition to her. She had jumped at the chance to earn the million dollars, which she was to get if she won or lost. She was a top flight whore, but she wanted out of the life. He had had, at the time, second thoughts about asking her to do it, but she was the only young, beautiful, ponygirl sized, former track star that he knew. Although he promised he would do everything he could to get her back once she had finished her job, he had told her that there was the risk that he might fail. She was satisfied at his pledge and was willing to take the risk. Well, now the then theoretical risk was real.

He sauntered over to where Giorgi's slave girl assistant was kneeling patiently in the dirt, awaiting her master's command. She wasn't his usual girl. Ilona, his pretty, blond slave girl, had been sold to Dr. Kevsky, for 20 thousand zlotskis, about $5,000.00. This new girl, whose skin was as black as the ace of spades, was unfamiliar to Jake. Nonetheless, when he sat down on one of the adult sized chairs that Giorgi kept out for guests, she immediately asked him, in a sharply twanged, inner city accent, whether he wanted anything to drink.

"Gin, if you have it," Jake replied. "If not, vodka."

The naked girl ran over to a table that had been set up amongst the revelers and returned with a liter sized bottle of domestic vodka, about 150 proof, and a small, shiny glass in the other. She set the bottle and glass on the table next to Jake and then knelt before him. "Shall I serve you, master?"

Jake knew that she was offering one of her other talents besides waitressing. He declined. But he was tempted. Her body was shiny black with broad, pinkish lips and a doll like face. Her curly hair was cut close cropped to her head. Her breasts danced nicely on her chest when she moved and had stiff, conical tips, tinged a slight pink. Her thighs and legs were slender and graceful. She was thin and small of stature, perhaps a little taller than the dwarf whom she served.

"No, thank you," Jake answered, pretending he did not catch her reference to a sexual service. "I'll pour my own." He squinted at the blue lettering tattooed across her chest. The two inch high, blue lettering had been highlighted faintly in red to make it stand out against the coal black skin. Jake had gotten good at deciphering the Cyrillic alphabet. "Shakira," he added once he had decoded it.

He poured out a couple of finger's worth of the firewater and downed it in one gulp. A wave of heat permeated his body as the liquor's effects went through him.

The girl went back to her previous perch. The crowd of men were rowdy and calling impassioned encouragement, in Russian, to Giorgi as he sawed his member back and forth between Chocolate's lips. They were the only part of her head or face that was visible. The dwarf groaned in reply, smiling broadly at his friends and, by the increase of the tempo of his thrusts, Jake discerned that he was near to climax.

Jake was clearly an outsider to this rough crowd. His presence was ignored like that of a pimple on someone's nose. You saw it, but who wanted to look at it. The girl, Shakira, was kept dashing to and fro between the men. Here and there one of them would caress her taut, round, black ass, or squeeze one of her apple sized breasts. Obediently, the girl allowed the familiarities. Jake knew, as the girl undoubtedly did too, that since Chocolate would be off limits to any other but Giorgi while there was still a race to be run, she would undoubtedly be very busy in a little while.

Suddenly, Giorgi gave out a loud grunt. His hands had been on the ponygirl's ample shoulders. Now they shifted to her head, which he clamped tightly between them. "Ohhhhhhh! Ohhhhhhh!" he moaned as his juices flowed down into the pony's belly. "Ohhhhh!" The assembled congratulators issued loud, raucous and ribald commemorations of the blessed event. Jake's cock twinged in jealousy. He knew first hand that the ponygirl was well accomplished at sucking a prick.

Giorgi let his climax run its course. He was still wearing his colorful racing uniform, gold and black like Chocolate's hood. When he was done, he slowly drew his softening manhood from between the former whore's lips and tucked it back into his pants. He saw Jake for the first time.

"Ah, Jake," he yelled. "I'm sorry, no fucking for Chocolate yet. Tomorrow, when we win, they'll be lined up like sailors at a whorehouse," he said, nodding to his friends, "but I'll get you in early."

Now that Jake was recognized as a friend, and one who would qualify for a first round fuck with the, hopefully, victorious ponygirl, the men warmed up to him. He received several of their jealous salutes.

"No, that's not why I've come," Jake replied after acknowledging the gestures of amity.

Giorgi bent down and picked up Lightning's gag which was lying on the ground next to his chair. He brushed it off on his uniform pants to free it of dirt and he proffered it to the obedient slave girl, instructing her to apply it to the ponygirl's mouth. Jake saw his chance.

"No," he said. "Let me do it."

Giorgi looked up at him. "You? Why you?"

Jake had to come up with an excuse quickly.

"Well, there's always the chance that she will lose tomorrow and that this will be the last I'll see of her up close. After all, I'm responsible for bringing her here and you've had her all to yourself for weeks. I just want to hold onto those wonderful breasts. You know, for luck."

It wasn't an excuse that would survive cross examination, but it was the best Jake could do at short notice. He had forgotten that so many people would be hanging around the camp.

Giorgi smiled. "Sure! Why not?" He gave out an unpleasant sounding laugh and handed the infernal device to Jake. He then announced Jake's offer to the others, who also laughed. The man next to him slapped him on the back and pronounced something to him in Russian.

Jake looked at Giorgi.

"He says that, if you're lucky, you'll get to fuck her all winter. And the other one too!"

It was understood that the man was referring to the equally desirable ponygirl, Lightning.

Giving back a weak smile, Jake got up from his chair and walked slowly over to where the ponygirl knelt. She was looking straight at him, although he could not see her eyes due to the small apertures in her hood. Keeping a ponygirl's vision diminished made her ability to discern what was going on around her extremely limited. It heightened her power to focus and raised all of her other senses to heightened abilities.

Chocolate had not seen Jake enter the camp site. "Jake!" she thought to herself with glee. It was a happy reminder that her time as a ponygirl would soon be coming to an end. She had done her job, won the gold medal. The race with the pony formerly known as Maddy would be on. Everything was going just as Jake had told her it would.

It had been hell being a ponygirl, especially in the beginning. Human beings got used to almost anything and the loss of her speech, the use of her arms, her constant nudity, had lost their impact. And in the last several weeks, at least, she had been away from the constant, promiscuous sexual use of her that had been her fate when she lived in the ponybarn. She merely had to submit to her driver's desires and to the handling of her by his pretty, blond slave girl. Soon, even that would be in the past. She knew exactly where she would move once she got the money, to a luxurious beach house overlooking the Pacific in Malibu. She had seen pictures of it in a magazine once.

And now, here was Jake. He had mainly stayed away from her during her training. She understood why. It would not due at all for the others to discover that she was a ringer in a scheme to rescue another ponygirl. It would mean certain death for Jake and, in all probability, a life of servitude as a formerly human beast for her. The prospect of being a ponygirl for life was one that she could not bear. It was only the fact that she knew it was temporary that had enabled her to endure it. A lifetime of sexual slavery, served as a silenced, facially anonymous beast, with fewer rights than a dog or a horse, was a prospect that made her shiver with fear. There were laws against mistreating dogs and horses. There were no such laws as far as ponygirls were concerned.

The pony who, beneath it all, still thought of herself as Jackie, opened her mouth readily when Jake proffered the gag to her lips. She could hear the undoubtedly rude comments of the other men in Russian as Jake dropped to a crouch in front of her. If he could have seen her face, he would have witnessed the brightening of her expression. Yes, even a smile.

Her coconspirator buckled the gag in place behind her head. As he leaned over, she could feel his shirt rub up against her stiffened nipples. She couldn't help it. Sucking the little man's cock had gotten her hot. Sucking almost any cock made her hot ever since she had been made into a ponygirl. Sex had become an obsession, just as her trainers had intended. Sure, she was used to fucking sometimes ten different men in a day when business was good back in Chicago. There had been even more when she was first broken in as a whore. And, after a while, she had come to enjoy some of it, especially when she knew that she had pushed her john into a paroxysm of pleasure beyond that he had known before. But this was different. Now, she craved it, craved the feel of its soft hardness against her tongue, its hot, heavy presence in her mouth. It was a stark contrast with the thick, inert, cold wad of leather that usually filled it. And she loved its rigid insistence at her gates of pleasure, usually bringing her a wave of ecstasy unlike any she had known before.

When Jake had finished affixing her gag, He leaned back and looked her in the eyes. His hands took hold of her breasts and squeezed them gently. She felt like she was going to melt. His hands were strong and hot. She had already promised herself that when she was liberated, she would fuck Jake for a week without stopping, first thing.

Then, she noticed that Jake was trying to say something to her. He was speaking low, almost in a whisper. He had his back to the other men so they could not see his lips move.

"Jackie," he said. "I've got to tell you something. Don't do anything to give us away. I have bad news. I just found out today that Burnham has betrayed us. If you lose the race tomorrow, you won't be going home, ever. The other estate will become your new owner. I'll never be able to free you. You've got to run like the devil himself tomorrow! Your whole life depends on it!"

The ponygirl, former whore, prospective millionaire, was stunned. How could this be? This wasn't part of the deal! She was supposed to go home, win or lose! Jake had promised! Then his words came back to her. He had said that he would be dealing with rough customers and might not be able to protect her. She had responded that she would take her chances as long as he promised to do his best.

"Oh, god!" she thought. A pit opened up in her belly. Her body ran cold and she began to shiver. To be a ponygirl for life was a thought she couldn't bear. What would happen to her when she was too old to run? What would they do with her then? And new owners? How would they treat her? And never to talk or use her hands again, to have her face denied the light of day, to have it become unfamiliar even to herself! It was too horrible to think of.

"Now, I know that this is terrible news, Jackie, but if the men find out I've been talking to you, there'll be hell to pay. The only way out is for you to win the race. If you do, I have everything set up. Win and I'll take you home. I promise."

Yes, Jackie thought. "Win! I have to win! I can do it! I have to do it!"

Jake gave her breasts a hard squeeze of reassurance. "You can do it Jackie! I know you can! Win, and in a few days, you'll be home."

Jake rose from his crouch and returned to his seat. He ignored the randy jokes from the other men and smiled weakly at Giorgi. "Just like I remembered them," he said. "I can't wait till tomorrow."

He stayed a while longer so as to make it appear that his visit was normal and routine. He downed several more shots of vodka. He kept a careful, if surreptitious eye on Jackie, to make sure that she was exhibiting no signs of having had any communication with him. She just knelt there stoically, her expressionless face hiding what he knew had to be turmoil inside her brain.

The diminutive driver curtly ordered his slave girl to mount Chocolate on the heavy wooden post in the middle of the encampment, kneeling down so that she could rest her wounded leg.

"Has Dr. Kevsky been out to see her?" Jake asked, trying to appear nonchalant.

"Right after the race," Giorgi answered. "I don't know about the ponygirl doctor's methods, but they seem to have worked in Chocolate's case. The slave girl will be getting her off a few times later. To 'relax the muscles', as the beautiful doctor has prescribed."

"Speaking of slave girls," Jake interjected, "when did you get the new one?"

"Oh, she's not mine," Giorgi said. "She belongs to a friend and is just on loan. I've been meaning to get a beautiful, black slave girl for a while. Now that Ilona's gone, I thought I'd try one out. She's marvelous, and well trained. Mr. Burnham promised me one of the Haitian girls that came in last week, black as night, if I win the race tomorrow."

Jake watched the black girl scurrying to and fro, serving Giorgi's guests. She was beautiful, and her shiny, black skin seemed to promise hours of delight. He hadn't known about the Haitian girls. Burnham's tentacles were spreading wider and wider. "Well, his world will come crashing down if I am able to get Maddy and Jackie out," Jake thought. Once the ruling authorities discovered the double game he played, Jake was certain that Burnham's remains would fertilize the vast Kalikastani plains somewhere.

He took a last look at the pony called Chocolate before he left. Her future was in her own hands, or too be more accurate, in her own feet. He had delivered the message. The rest was up to her.

* * * * * * * * * * * * * *

It was a very suspicious Irkut who watched Jake leave the camp. He was standing about 20 yards up the service road and had seen everything. What had had seen, and Giorgi had not, was the movement of Jake's lips. "He's talking to her!" Irkut exclaimed to himself. "I can't believe it! I was right! Something's going on!" What it was, he couldn't tell, but you didn't talk to a ponygirl unless you had some idea of freeing her. Was that why they wanted to own Lightning? Was that what this was all about? But why Lightning amongst all the other former women who now served as ponies? What was the connection? He would have to find out. No one would believe him unless he showed some kind of motive, after all, Burnham was a very important man in Kalikastan now. Taking him down would mean the loss of hundreds of millions of dollars. When he discovered the connection, he would put an end to the Americans' schemes nonetheless

* * * * * * * * * * * * * *

As promised, Jake delivered himself to Tanya's mother's campsite within the prescribed period of time. The blond haired beauty gleefully welcomed him. The campsite was full of activity. Tanya's mother, Helena, had apparently decided not to wait for the outcome of the claiming race between Lightning and Chocolate the next morning to begin the trek back to her estate. Her other two daughters and her four shapely and enticing, naked slave girls were scurrying around gathering things up. One of her sons, Ivan, was loading her ponies, one by one, into the large transportation trailer.

The ponies had had their racing hoods removed and now wore hoods of dark green, their fiery, red ponytails extending out of the backs. The welts from their post-loss beatings had already started to fade. Tanya's mom was not overly cruel and she was, in fact, proud of how well her six Irish lovelies had performed. So she had apparently been light on them. As Jake watched Ivan lead the pony known as Molly to the trailer, he felt a pang of disappointment that he had never had the chance to try her out. His days of fucking ponygirls, or slave girls for that matter, were rapidly coming to a close. He would miss it.

Dr. Kevsky was also having her trailer loaded. Tanya's other brother was helping her out. On the ground, waiting to be loaded, sat six tiny cages with delectable feminine flesh stuffed in each one. These were the rewards of the ponygirl doctor's assistance to Chocolate. Jake knew two of the girls, Ilona, of course, Giorgi's former servant, and the Malaysian girl known as Orchid. Ilona had responded well to the doctor, one might even say adoringly, while the doctor had been in Giorgi's camp. Jake wondered whether she felt the same way now. The cage was so small that the bars pressed in firmly on her skin. She was kneeling with her torso bent over, her bare, mammary plentitude pressed onto her thighs. Her wrists were locked behind her and her ankles were joined together. Her head was jutted out forwards, fixed upon a thick leather gag that protruded from the inside of the cage into her distended mouth. Another thick, leather prong was implanted in her rear, pinning the slave girl in place. The girl was literally unable to move a muscle in her harsh confinement. Jake saw her cast a forlorn, sideways glance at him with one eye. A single tear floated down her cheek from it.

The Malaysian girl looked just as unhappy. In fact, all of them did. The four lovely girls who had been used in Burnham's entertainment the other night were there, looking especially dismayed. Their eyes flitted about frantically and their faces conveyed their disbelief that anyone would confine them in such a cruel and heartless way. They had not had the opportunity to experience any slave training as of yet, other than what they had received, ad hoc, over the last few days. Undoubtedly, they had all been given a good sample of what slave girl life was like, but that would not really prepare them for the rigors of slave training, which Jake knew to be quite harsh. It had to be to produce the compliant, sexually obedient creatures that populated the estates and whorehouses of the country.

Dr. Kevsky had indicated that her brand of training regimen was especially harsh. It had to be pretty bad to deserve that sobriquet. He looked at the unhappy face of the Malaysian girl. He had hoped that he was saving her from Burnham's cruel depredations by recommending that Dr. Kevsky ask for her as part of the price for her services to Chocolate. Now, he wondered whether he had pulled her from the frying pan and dropped her into the fire.

The doctor emerged from her trailer as Jake was finishing his inspection of the six prospective victims of the doctor's brand of sadism.

"Jake," she exclaimed, "I'm so happy to see you before we leave. I'm sorry I can't stay for the race tomorrow, but as you see, I have my hands full. The sooner the creatures begin their training the better."

Jake had a rush of desire as he recalled his session with the sexually voracious doctor the night before. Tanya was clinging to his arm, and she noticed it right away. "Don't blush, Jake," she teased him. "You'll get to see a lot of Svetlana once we get married. I'll bet that she'll even give you a tour of her slave school. It's always good to have an extra cock around to give the girls some practical experience."

"Oh, yes, Jake," the doctor exclaimed. "You have to come."

Jake knew that that was impossible. Either he would be out of the country within forty eight hours or be dead trying. So it didn't hurt to promise anything.

"I'll make a point of it," he answered. "But why send Ilona through another slave training course? She's been a slave girl a long time. She knows the ropes only too well by now."

"Well, I've decided that she will become one of my house slaves and it wouldn't do for the other ones to be fully trained under my system and not her," Svetlana responded. "I think that she'll benefit from it. One of our specialties is what you might call 'tune ups' of girls who have been somewhat slack in their obligations. Ilona is a wonderful slave girl, but she'll be so much more fastidious in her duties when I'm through with her."

All of this was said within earshot of the unfortunate girl. Boris had begun loading the other girls' cages into the trailer.

"Why such close confinement?" Jake asked. He knew that nothing he could say or do would lessen the girls' hardships, but he did want to make note of his sensibilities on the subject.

"My system is based on total compliance, as are most of the other training systems," the doctor answered. "In my system, we start from the imposition of total immobility of the subject. Each increment of freedom of movement has to be earned. This is just the start."

"Oh," was all Jake was able to say.

"My system also differs in that it's based on a type of self training. Once a slave girl progresses beyond the confinement stage, she then becomes responsible for training a new girl coming in. If she fails to get her trainee to progress sufficiently, she's put back where she started. It's a marvelously effective system and one that needs little supervision. The slave center practically runs itself. Each level is trained by the one just higher than it. In the last stage, the girls are trained by myself and the staff directly, but little work is required on them by that time."

Boris, a strapping youth, picked up Ilona's cage by a handle at its top with one hand. Ilona gave out a muffled squeal as her body shifted ever so slightly in her prison. Jake wondered whether he should say goodbye to her, but thought better of it.

"You should send us one or two of your current girls, Jake. You won't recognize them when they come back," the doctor told him.

The doctor's invitation made Jake think of his personal slave girl, Dana, back at Burnham's estate. He obviously could not take her with him when he left the country. If he were staying around, he might just have sent her to the doctor's facility. Dana was a good whore, but there was a surliness in her obedience sometimes that affronted him. He had not been able to beat it out of her. Well, that would be someone else's problem now.

"Jake, let's let Dr. Kevsky get on with her tasks. I've got a nice dinner planned and then we can retire for some languorous delight. I'll show you everything that Svetlana has taught me."

The beautiful physician laughed. "That will take some time, Jake. I hope that you don't expect to have any time for sleeping." She and Tanya laughed.

The dinner that Tanya had arranged for was served inside the tent that had been the scene of their debauchery the night before. It was made up nicely with flowers and the table was set down near the floor with them both sitting cross legged in front of it on the same side.

All during the meal, Tanya kept stealing kisses and giving Jake warm, lascivious caresses. They were served by two of Tanya's mother's pretty, naked, little slave girls. Although her mother was leaving, her father was not and he would take them and the tent home.

Tanya made sure that Jake had an ample inspection of their attributes, their soft, full breasts, their tender, hairless slits, as if he needed additional encouragement to his libido. They were delightful. Jake asked Tanya if they had been trained by Dr. Kevsky.

"Of course," Tanya replied. The girls wore tattoos of a voracious, yet sensuous, black panther on their lower bellies, the emblem, he assumed, of the doctor's training center. Jake had to admit that there was something special about their demeanor and the anxiousness in which they sought to please the diners that set them apart. He wondered, idly, what it would be like to fuck them.

The dinner's first course was a hot lentil soup flavored by locally grown nuts and herbs. There was a second serving of large, Black Sea prawns and then medallions of beef covered in a white mushroom sauce. When the remnants of the last course had been taken away by the slave girls, Tanya announced, "I'm for dessert," and pulled him to the soft, rug covered floor.

CHAPTER FOUR

In another section of the Tournament grounds, in a luxurious tent of the kind reserved for the owners and trainers, Anton Drabik was sitting, naked and morose, in a camp chair, a half filled glass of vodka in his hand. He too was spending the evening in the company of a female, but one of a very different type than the beautiful, free woman, Tanya. Swinging from one of the overhead poles, her hands bound to her ankles, was the Italian slave girl Antonia. Her thighs were spread wide, revealing her much abused slit and the tiny, brown star of her rear entrance. She was blindfolded and was wearing a thick, leather gag that sported a ring on the outside. The ring, connected to her ankle and wrist ties above her, prevented her head from swinging down and eased, somewhat, the strain on her neck. Her thighs and pudenda were crisscrossed with the evidence of a recent whipping. The evil instrument that had produced her torment still lay in her new owner's left hand.

To the lovely, black haired slave girl, it seemed that she had been cast into the fires of hell itself. This man who now possessed her had a soul of fire, a vicious heart and an apparently conscienceless mind. He had owned her for two days and this was the third time he had beaten her. Each time was worse than the last. She had been beaten often while she was being retrained, and for her failure to attract a buyer while she was being held for sale, but those sojourns had been bearable because she knew that they were temporary. Now that she was owned by a master, her status was, more or less, permanent. How she would survive days and days of endless suffering, she didn't know.

The muscles of her shoulders ached severely from the strain of the weight of her body on them. Her pussy and thighs burned from her recent whipping. Her throat was raw from her screams of pain. What had she ever done that made her deserve a fate like this, she thought woefully. She could not see her tormentor, but she knew that he was still there. Her ears were finely tuned to the sounds of his movements and she dreaded the sound of him rising from his perch to resume her abuse.

If only she had the means to end her own life, she would do it. She didn't have the courage to get the man to beat her to death through acts of defiance or disobedience. The thought of the pain she would have to bear was too much. She had vowed that as soon as the opportunity arose, a knife left unattended, a truck passing by at a time when she was not tethered or bound into immobility, a chance to leap off of a high place, she would take it.

There was always the opportunity to go on a hunger strike, to not eat until she withered away and died. One of the girls in the center where she had been retrained had tried that. The men had merely shoved a tube down her throat and forced her to consume the chalky tasting gruel that served as the slave girls' repast. And then she was severely beaten. The next feeding period, she hastily downed the offering and licked the bowl clean.

On the other hand, when the man had fucked her, it felt like her pussy had been set aflame. He fucked her with hard, cruel strokes of his thick cock like he was wielding a steely weapon. The last time, just before he hauled her up to her current grotesque, cruel position, she had screamed out her pleasure long and loud. It was like every cell in her body had been brought to life by her ordeals. Even now, swaying from the roof pole of the tent, her wrists and ankles burning from the burden they supported, her body felt like it was aglow.

She didn't want to be whipped, she didn't want to be raped by the dark, foreboding male who had the power of life and death over her, but her body seemed to be overruling her mind. Maybe this total emersion in the experience of her degradation was the only route of escape for her. She would become a being crazed by the need for punishment until she was able to satisfy her yearning for oblivion by forcing her abuser past the point of no return. As much as her body seemed to crave the man's heinous attentions, though, her conscious mind still feared and dreaded the resumption of her travail. She was trying not to cry, trying not to give in to hopelessness and despair, but she couldn't suppress the doleful sob that welled up in her. Her muffled voice resounded through the deathly silent tent.

The sound shook Drabik from his alcohol besotted trance. He had been contemplating his own black heart. The faces of the men and women he had dispatched so callously so many times, the slaves he had punished and tortured, the females he had broken to the bit.

The killer had been searching his soul for the source of his entrancement with the ponygirl Lightning. There was no rationality in it. She was, except for her superior racing abilities, just like all the other ponygirls. Something in her had reached that last spark of humanity within him, bringing out that which he had deemed lost forever.

He knew that he could not live on this way. He had to stamp out the simmering ashes of his soul. There was only one way to do that: the ponygirl had to die, and at his hands. He had to squeeze the life out of her, extinguish the spark of her being. He had tried everything else.

He looked at the dark haired slave girl dangling from the roof of his tent. For now, her body would be the focus of all his lusts, desires and, yes, hatred. He hated what the ponygirl had made of him. He hated his need for her. At the same time, he could not deny it.

Drabik stood and stepped over to the hanging, young girl. He chugged back the dregs of his vodka and tossed the glass aside. The girl's body seemed to shiver as the sound of his movements reached her and he heard her give out a little moan of unhappiness.

The dark, unhappy man moved himself until he was positioned in front of the girl's forced open thighs. He placed his hand on her protruding posterior and gave her body a little shove. She swung helplessly away and then back towards him. As she did, she uttered a squeal of pain though her gag. He let her continue to sway back and forth, pendulum like, until her body finally came once more to rest. His eyes were on the red lined pussy so open and inviting to him. He placed his hand on it and delved his thumb between the wounded lips. When he reached the nubbin at its top, the girl's body stiffened and he thought he heard her utter the word 'no' miserably, deep in her throat.

He continued to trace the divide between the slave girl's nether lips, pausing each time at her stiffening clit to administer a caress, for about a minute, or until the girl's canal had begun to secrete the juices of her arousal and his thumb was able to gain easy access to her soft, hot interior.

He began to fuck her with it, pressing the bulbous digit deeply into her crevasse and then out again in a slow, rhythmic motion. At the end of each outward stroke, he spread the moisture that his thumb had gathered and smeared it over the girl's pleasure button. Soon, she began to moan. Her thighs shifted slightly as if she was straining to close them, either to deny him access to her pot of pleasure, or to capture the hand that tormented her and to drive it deeper within.

Actually, Antonia did not know what she would have preferred had she been able to bring her knees together. Her mind wanted his abuse of her sex to stop, to be free of his rude hands, to determine for herself who did and did not have the right to administer these caresses. Her body, though, was urging the man's hand on, yearning for deliverance into that zone where her physical sensations obliterated her conscious thoughts. Pleasure or pain, it was all the same. Either would drive out the mind that mourned her reduction to a chattel, a thing to be bought and sold, make her forget the plain looking, young, plump girl who had loved her and who she had loved in return.

The odor of the girl's arousal wafted its way to Drabik's nose, fuelling his lust. The girl's sex was a little more than shoulder high to him and it was an easy thing to lean over and substitute his tongue and his lips for his hand. He gave her clit a long, hard suckle, causing a moan to emanate from her, a moan, he knew, of pleasure. He drew his tongue down the lines of her engorged labia, and then up again, only to tease and torment the hard button of flesh at their apex.

The man was wild with lust. He pressed his lips over the girl's clit and sucked hard while dragging his hot tongue over her sensitive point. The girl's moans became louder and her thighs began to twitch. Suddenly, she gave out a deep groan and her body began to contort and shake as if she had been pierced by a fierce jolt of electricity.

Antonia could feel the man's hands on her soft, embattled thighs and their heat accelerated her passion. His tongue tormented her clit remorselessly. She felt her mind slip away and accede to her body's demand for pleasure. "Mmmmmmmmmpf! Mmmmmmmmmpf!" she moaned as her orgasm wracked her. The sharp, intense contractions of her canal sent waves of unbearable pleasure all through her. Her hands strained sat her bindings, her back arched, her knees shook and wavered.

Drabik was not satisfied with one explosion of lust from the girl. He drove her on and on until she was screaming her pleasure into the dimly lit tent. She was sobbing and moaning, her body jerking as if she was on the end of a string and someone was yanking her up and down.

His lusts were driving him to his own oblivion. His cock was hard as stone and pulsed with his need. He could hold himself back no more and he withdrew his lips and tongue from the girl's drenched and pulsating quim. He reached for the chain that held her body aloft and, disconnecting it from the central pole, lowered her until her pussy was level with his rampant meat. He locked the chain back off again and, seizing her thighs, drove her hard down on his pole. He heard her gasp as he penetrated her. Her pussy was hot and welcomed his invading cock by clamping down on it. Drabik had no time to waste. He pistoned his rigid piece back and forth in the lubricated hole, the friction driving his needs higher and higher. When his cock exploded, he yelled out, "Ahhhhhhhhhhhrg!" and he felt his essence jetting down his meat and into the belly of his captive. His hips pounded against the girl's thighs as he tried to slam himself deeper and deeper within her. She groaned with pleasure and her cunt spasmed, squeezing his weapon again and again.

Once his forces were exhausted, Drabik let his softening cock slip from the girl's pussy. His cock was red from its exertions. For the moment, his blood was cooled.

In his lust, he had discarded the long, thin whip that he had beaten her with earlier. He ignored it, momentarily, and instead retrieved his discarded glass. He poured himself another two inches of the potent liquor and downed it in one gulp. And then another. It was going to be a long night. The race was more than twelve hours away. She had to win, she just had to, or his obsession with her would never die, he thought, madly. He went to the door of his tent and stared out into the dark night. She was out there, less than a half mile away. Her driver had undoubtedly put his clammy, little dwarf's hands on her and soiled her once more with his spewm. If she lost tomorrow, this would be the last night of the little man's life. That was for sure. And, in less than forty eight hours, that bastard Grobgy would join him in hell.

The peace and relief that his orgasm had given him lasted no more than a few minutes. His ire rose rapidly. He looked back in the tent at the softly moaning, naked slave girl. Her body was still swaying gently back and forth. He tossed aside his glass once more, leaned over, and picked up his whip.

* * * * * * * * * * * * * * *

Not 50 yards from where the Italian slave girl suffered, another slave girl was going through her own torments. This was at the hands of Grobgy's beautiful daughter,

Anya. She, too, was filled with ire and self loathing. The source of her bedevilment was the man, Anton Drabik. He had fucked her roundly in the stairwell outside the owner's' clubhouse yesterday, but she had not been able to spend a single, private moment with him since. He had promised that they would get together two days hence at their little hideaway about 30 miles from her father's estate, but that was not enough. She wanted all of the dark, brooding enforcer. She didn't want to share him with anyone, especially not with that slut of a ponygirl.

In Anya's right hand was a long, thin whip, much like the one that was being wielded by Anton Drabik back in his tent. The slave girl was kneeling on the thick rug, her head pressed down on it, her hands locked behind her back. The backs of her thighs and her dainty rear end were exposed to her cruel mistress's depredations.

Angelique had been a slave girl for about ten months. She was a native of Brussels and had been caught out late one night with two of her girlfriends by a gang of youths near the factory district. They had brought the girls to their hideout located in the bowels of an abandoned factory where the girls were raped and then locked into little cages. A man had come by a few days later and bought them.

Prior to her current duties as the evil Anya's personal body slave, she had worked in the Grobgy mansion performing light cleaning duties and making herself available to Grobgy's men or the gangster's frequent guests. It hadn't been too bad, as slave assignments go. She only had to fuck maybe two or three times a day and give out a few blow jobs here and there. Grobgy's men usually saved their worst for the girls who were lodged in their bunkhouse.

The black haired slave girl stood all of 5'3" in her high heels back in Brussels. She had narrow, sweet, hips, small, apple sized breasts and lips that set out in a heavy pout. Her face was pretty, her features well proportioned. Her only defect was a small mole on her chin.

Angelique had been filled with dread when she was selected by Anya to be her new body slave. She had only worked for her for two days and already she had been beaten twice. And while well trained in the Sapphic arts, if she had to be a sex slave, she definitely preferred cock to muff. Nonetheless, she had given her mistress oral relief five or six times already, all while being denied any relief of her own. Even while alone, she was kept in a little cage in Anya's tent, her hands bound behind her, so that she could not attend to her own needs. She hoped and prayed that her assignment was temporary.

Anya raised the long, thin whip and brought it down swiftly across the backs of Angelique's thighs. The girl gave out a high pitched squeak, long and loud. She didn't want to cry out, but she couldn't help it. It hurt like hell.

A narrow line of red appeared along the tender tissue, joining four others that Anya had put there just moments ago.

"Have you had enough, slut?" she yelled at the tiny girl. "Or do you need five more?"

"N,no, mistress! Please, no more! Please! I'll be g-good! I p-promise!" Angelique stammered back desper-ately. Tears were flowing from her pretty little eyes. Five blows from the whip was about all she could take without becoming a blithering pool of hysteria. The five on the back of her thighs matched the five that her mistress had laid across her doll like breasts and her taut belly during her two prior whippings.

Angelique hardly knew what sin she had committed. It had something to do with the way she had looked at her mistress, or put away the blouse that she had been wearing, or poured her tea. One of those three, she wasn't sure. Whichever it was, she would do better at all three next time.

"Stay where you are, cunt," Anya spat out. She was wearing a long, silken robe covered with a fine Japanese print. When pressed up against her skin, it looked almost translucent. The gangster's daughter was not yet ready for bed. She was changing so that she could go to her father's post tournament party. And, she was expecting someone. Someone important.

Although she was expecting company, the cute derriere of the tiny slave girl was too much to resist. She went to the steamer trunk that she used when at the tournament and pulled from one of its drawers a long, thick, black, strap on dildo. It was one of her favorites and one that she had yet to introduce her new servant to. She quickly opened her robe and strapped it on. It had a battery inside and when she pressed the button, it produced a vibration up and down the length of the stiff, shiny instrument, one that caused the knob that rested against her clit to deliver an exquisite sensation to her loins. She took a dab of lubricant from a small jar in the drawer and covered the tip of the faux prick with it. It wasn't that she was afraid of causing the young thing pain. Quite the contrary. It was just that she didn't want to tear her all up. She didn't want the girl sidelined by a need for medical attention already. She had just gotten her.

The slave girl could not see what her mistress was up to, but she made a good guess. The other slave girls had told her about the collection of dildos possessed by the young woman, some of them designed to deliver, not pleasure, but pain. Her belly felt queasy as she waited to find out which one her mistress was going to use tonight. Whichever it was, she knew that she had to bear it. The girls had also told her that there was a rumor that Anya's last body slave, Natalie, had been buried alive somewhere for pissing her off. Angelique didn't know if it was true, but she wasn't taking any chances. Just the thought of it was horrifying.

The tall, lanky, well built woman, the black prong protruding proudly from her loins, knelt behind the diminutive girl. The vibrations of the devise were already getting Anya randy. When you added the thought of dominating this wisp of a creature, accentuating her submissive, enslaved state, it really got her hot!

Anya pressed the tip of the plastic prick against the small girl's narrow, brown star. The girl moaned as the bulbous head stretched the tissue. The vibrations sent a familiar feeling through her loins. At last, she thought, a chance to get off.

Anya had just fitted the thick, round head into the girl's rear when there was a knocking on one of the tent poles that formed the door to her portable boudoir. "Shit!" she said to herself. It was important though, more important than cornholing this little whore.

Anya reached for the belt to the device and unhooked it from her waist. She drew herself back from it, leaving it humming and vibrating in the young slave's ass. "In a moment," she called out to her visitor. Before she rose to her feet, she pushed the dildo the rest of the way in so that it was fully immersed in the girl's bowels.

After regaining her feet, Anya pulled her robe closed round her and tied off the sash. "Come in," she called out.

The man who entered was dressed all in black. He had a greasy face, a dullard's brow and cruel, beady eyes. He was shorter than Anya by at least a foot.

"You sent for me, Miss Grobgy," the man snarled out, eyeing the display of Anya's charms through her form fitting, flimsy robe.

The gangster's daughter gave out a little shudder of disgust. "Is everything set for tonight?" she asked, haughtily. "Can you do it?"

"Of course, miss," the man replied. His face broke into a sinister smile. He looked down and saw the little slave girl, the dildo protruding from her rear. "Did I interrupt something, Miss Grobgy," he asked leeringly.

"That's none of your affair Gregor. Just tend to your business and you'll be well paid," she snapped back.

Gregor swept past the regal young woman and crouched down so that he could see the slave girl better. He reached for the vibrating dildo and slowly drew it in and out of the small hole.

Angelique was being driven mad by the vibrating in her rear. She, like most of the slave girls, had learned to get off from getting ass fucked and her pussy was beginning to drip with her arousal. But the vibrations alone would not do it; they just caused her to burn with unfulfilled desire. She was mortified that the man, whoever he was, had seen her posed so obscenely with the instrument of her ravishment protruding from her. You would think that the slave girls would get used to the humiliation of being unable to govern who used them and how, but they never did. Not really. Angelique was no exception.

"I think that maybe a little bonus might be in order, Miss Grobgy," the abhorrent looking man said. "After all, we'll be sharing a very important secret after tonight."

Anya quailed at the thought of being in the man's power. She would, of course, have him killed as soon as possible after the job was done. For now, though, she had to keep him satisfied.

"You can have her, later tonight, after the job's done," Anya said.

The man took hold of Angelique's hair at the back of her head and pulled her face up. The slave girl moaned with the pain of having her torso supported by her hair. She looked at the man who was abusing her and gasped. Was her mistress giving her to him! Oh, that couldn't be! She mustn't! He was revolting looking and coarse and his face bespoke a primitive cruelty. "Oh my god!" she thought. "No!"

"She looks pretty enough," Gregor said, his eyes drinking in the young girl's mien, her dainty little breasts, her fragile, little girl's hands locked behind her back. "I'll bet she howls when her titties are pinched," he said. A line off saliva dripped from the corner of his mouth. Angelique trembled with unhappiness.

"Come back later and you can have her," Anya said. "But let me tell you one thing. If you think that what you're doing puts me in your power, you're mistaken. If you ever said anything to anyone about this you would be sealing your own doom. And it wouldn't be pleasant. My father may get mad at me, but I doubt that he would do to me what he would do to you. So just think about that. With this slave girl, you'll be paid in full. Got that?"

"Oh, yesssss, Miss Grobgy," the man hissed. "And paid very well indeed. I've never owned my own slave girl before. It will be lots of fun."

Angelique started to cry. "Oh god, please don't let it happen, please!" she thought.

Gregor released Angelique's hair and her head fell to the carpet. He stood. "I'll see you in a few hours, miss," he snarled. "Don't forget your promise."

"I won't," Anya replied.

The grotesque looking man slinked from the tent. Anya's heart quickened its beat. If all went well, Lightning would surely lose the race tomorrow. She was exhilarated. She turned to the slave girl who still knelt on the carpet. "Just what I need!" she thought. She opened her robe and knelt again behind her. Once she had the dildo restrapped to her waist, its shuddering knob resting against her clit, she placed her hands on the girl's narrow, graceful hips and began to stroke the stiff, plastic intruder slowly back and forth in her small entrance. "Ahhhh," she moaned.

Despite her dismay at her dismal future, within a few moments, Angelique was giving off moans of her own.

* * * * * * * * * * * * * *

The brawny American billionaire who had started all these events in motion, was in his own trailer and in the midst of abusing one of his favorite victims. It was the bird-like Betty, his former secretary, symbol, to him, of all the limitations and confinements that he had left behind. Michael Burnham had had the fortyish bird-woman cleaned up and brought back to him for the evening. She was, obediently, kneeling on all fours on his sumptuous bed her hind parts towards him. They had been at if for over an hour. Betty had fresh crop marks across her thighs and breasts and her throat was still sore from having her former employer's thick cock shoved down it.

Burnham was sitting up in bed, his back to the headboard. A glass of neat, single malt scotch was in his left hand. He was, as was Betty, of course, naked, and his well used prick was, for the moment, laying dormant across his thigh. He had his right hand between Betty's creamy, white thighs, a stark contrast to the bright red, green, yellow and blue feather-like tattoos that covered her upper body from the top of her hair depleted skull to her waist. For now, the plastic, yellow beak that Burnham had had made up for her was lying on the floor. Burnham would reinstall it before he locked her into her cage for the night.

"So, how are you enjoying the tournament, Betty?" he asked her. Betty's real name was Elizabeth and, when she had been his executive secretary, she had been known as Liz. She now had the more pedestrian name, Betty, stenciled in deep blue across her chest and wore, as did all of Burnham's other slave girls, at least the ones that came through his slave training academy, a fierce black mastiff, with blood red fangs and eyes, etched permanently onto her belly.

Betty was hard put to answer her master. She was panting heavily as a result of the man's exercise of her plush, fur covered canal, tottering on the edge of another orgasm. Her wrists were confined in front of her by a chain that passed through a ring on her slave collar. When she stood, it forced her elbows to jut out like little wings. Now, they were implanted down on the bed.

""G-good, master," Betty replied. As if she would say anything else to the man who had destroyed her life and made her into a monster. In fact, Betty had spent almost all of her waking time attached to a post outside Burnham's huge trailer a sign next to her advertising free blow jobs. Burnham had had a ring gag installed in her mouth so that she could not refuse anyone. She must have given more than seventy five blow jobs a day for the three days. The number would undoubtedly have been more had not pussy been a dime a dozen during the festival. Nonetheless, her exotic mien was sufficiently novel for men who were otherwise sated to want to belly up and have their cranks sucked by a giant bird. All they had to do was separate the top half of her soft plastic beak from the bottom and her mouth awaited them, forced into a cock sized circle.

Burnham had no real interest in how Betty enjoyed the festival beyond knowing that she had suffered extreme torments and humiliation. It was her punishment for betraying him. She had taken home to her New York apartment copies of a number of sensitive documents as insurance in case the Feds ever brought a case against her for aiding Burnham in one of his corporate crimes. Burnham, after learning of it through a surreptitious search of her apartment by some of his agents, had lured "Liz" to Kalikastan where he had given her the choice of slavery or death. She had chosen slavery, as he knew she would, and she had been one of the focal points of his cruelty ever since.

"Don't lie to me bitch," Burnham snarled. His hand, which had been driving the bird woman's pleasure, now turned to pain as he grabbed her distended labia between his strong, thick fingers and gave them a mighty squeeze.

"Ohhhhhhhh!" Betty moaned. "Ohhhhhhhh!" It felt like someone had driven a sharp object into her loins. Tears started to flow anew down her painted cheeks. Her whole body cringed and she had to fight off the effort to draw her knees together. She knew better than to beg him to stop. Unsolicited verbiage from a slave girl was severely punished.

"Do you like it when I punish you, Betty? Is that it?"

"N-no master," the woman managed to eke out.

"Then why do you lie to me, eh?"

"I'm sorry, master! I'm sorry! It was terrible! It truly was!"

"And what did you learn from it, slut?"

"Never to betray my master, master! I'll never betray you again!"

Of course, in Betty's mind she had not betrayed anyone, but that was neither here nor there.

Burnham released his former secretary's quim and resumed his soft, careful stroking of it. Betty's body relaxed and, although her pussy lips still burned, allowed herself to enjoy the lust driving sensations. After all, coming was really the only pleasure that a slave girl had, be she aviary or otherwise.

"Yes," Burnham replied. "Never betray your master. I'm happy that the experience of sucking off over two hundred cocks in three days was a learning experience for you. Maybe some day I'll begin to feel that you have suffered enough for your crime against me."

"Yes, Master," Betty crooned. Her master's hand was stroking her stiffened clit and the trilling sensations were filtering throughout her body. Seven months ago, Betty had been a well endowed, lust inspiring, accomplished executive corporate assistant, but now she was a slave girl through and through. She took her pleasure where she could find it, even at the hands of the man she hated more than anyone in the whole world.

"Oh, I have something to tell you, Betty," Burnham added. "I've had an offer to sell you. Really! Do you want to hear more about it?"

After her recent painful experience, Betty decided that she might as well tell the truth.

"N-no master," she replied.

"Well, I'm going to tell you anyway, Betty, because I'm thinking of selling you. It seems a Japanese fellow is putting together a kind of circus. He's converted a couple of slave girls into cows with huge udders and freakish snouts. He has a pig lady and a girl who's been converted into a little fuck doggie. She's very cute. I saw her just yesterday. She has little tufts of auburn hair on her head and her face has been reshaped into a little doggie snout. She has a real working tail too and little doggie legs! I think he called her Lavender. He wants you in his circus. You'll be the bird woman and he'll teach you little bird like tricks. Won't that be fun?"

Burnham often came up with theoretical threats to do more humiliating things to her body so it was hard for Betty to know whether he was telling the truth or not. For once, though, he sounded like he meant it.

"No, master! Please don't sell me to him!" she whined.

"Oh, he's offered me a lot of money, Betty. You know that I find it hard to turn down money. I think that I'll actually be making a profit on you."

Betty just whined again. She had often wondered how her life could possibly be more miserable, and now she had an inkling of how.

"And there's more," Burnham announced. His hand had become very active between Betty's widespread legs and she was having a hard time following him, lost in her impending crisis.

"You know how I keep your hands locked up so that your elbows look like wings? Well, he's going to give you real wings. He's going to cut off your arms below the elbow and sew them into these feathered wings that he's constructed. As for your beak, he's going to make sure that it becomes a permanent part of your face, but still flexible enough so that you can suck cocks. What do you think of that, Betty?"

"N-noooooo, master, please...." Betty moaned. Her needs were building higher and higher. She didn't want to listen to the horrible things that Burnham was telling her, but she didn't want to miss the chance to orgasm again. Her hips were thrusting back at the hand that was manipulating her sex. Her full, multicolored breasts were tight with the blood of her excitement, her breath growing shorter and shorter.

"And best of all," Burnham went on, making sure that his stroking of her lustful slit continued, "he's going to remove your voice box and have a little device installed that will make you cackle like a bird every time that you try and talk. There's another device that he will implant in you so that every time he wants you to squawk he can press a button and it'll give you such a shock that you'll squawk like there's no tomorrow. How about that?"

"Oh, oh, oh, oh," Betty called out. Her orgasm was coming. It ran through her like a freight train. Her body contracted and her pussy convulsed. "Oh! Oh! Oh! Oh!" she screamed. "Ohhhhhhhhh!" Ohhhhhhhhh! Yes master, yes, don't stop master, please don't stop!"

She had forgotten what he was saying. It would register later though. It would tell her that she had to do something to get out of Kalikastan or die trying.

Once the tremors and spasms of her pussy ran down, her breathing began to return to normal. Her heart was beating like a drum in her chest. She had never had sex like that back in the States. It would be the one thing that she would miss.

Burnham gave her only a moment to recover her senses. "Enough play time, Betty. You've been neglecting your duties. I want you to turn around and take my cock in your mouth. If you don't have me good and hard in one minute, I'm going to give you another beating. So hop to it."

Frantic at the thought of another session with Burnham's riding crop, Betty spun around and captured Burnham's limp cock between her lips. He gave out a little, soft moan and leaned back.

"Tomorrow's the big day, Betty," he told her as she assiduously worked his tool. "If all goes well, I'll own the two fastest ponygirls in Kalikastan, probably the best in the world. Of all the people here, besides Jake and his men, you were the only other one to know that we were here to get Maddy. It's a good thing for you that you kept your mouth shut, so to speak. I don't think you can imagine the pain you would have suffered if I found out that you told anyone. After tomorrow, though, it won't matter. Once the Commission sees that I have no intent of setting Lightning or any other pony free, they'll know that there's no reason to worry. We can go on here for decades."

Burnham was lost in his reveries. He had been carrying these secrets with him for months. Once he had seen what was really going on in Kalikastan, all thoughts of saving Maddy had gone by the boards. But he had no one to talk to. He knew that Jake wouldn't stand for leaving Maddy and his chocolate colored friend, Jackie, as ponygirls. He would have to go.

"That Jake, he thinks that he has me fooled. Did you know that Betty?" Burnham continued. Betty knew who Jake was and what his mission was. She knew him from jobs he had done for Burnham back in the US before all of this had happened. She knew that he was getting Maddy out and she had made him promise to try and get her out too. That was the real reason she had kept quiet. For if she had ratted Burnham out, Jake would have been implicated and she would certainly still remain a slave. Her life with Burnham was bad, but, as she had just been reminded, it could be worse. With Jake, at least there was a chance for freedom. Her lips were paying service to Burnham's cock, but her ears were attuned to his words.

"He thinks that he's got me fooled," he went on, his hand stroking the bald head that was buried in his loins. "He told me that they plan to get Maddy and Jackie out a week or two after the tournament's over, but I know that that's bullshit. They're going to move the day after we get back. That's what I would do. I'm going to move first. Forty eight hours from now Jake and his crew will be lying under the steppes."

Panic went off in Betty's mind. Jake was her only hope at salvation! She had to get word to him somehow! Tomorrow! She had to talk to him tomorrow! She had to make sure that Burnham let her go watch the race, then she'd have a chance to see Jake.

The birdwoman didn't miss a stroke of her lips along Burnham's fat, limp cock. It was just starting to fill with blood. A chill went through her body as she heard her master say, "Ten seconds left, Betty."

CHAPTER FIVE

The next morning was as bright and pleasant a day as you might ever find in Kalikastan. It seemed that the second summer would last one more day. It was as if the god of ponygirl racing had intervened so that the historic match between the two American ponygirls would have a proper setting.

The crowd had begun to fill the stands early. Many of them had packed up their gear so that when the race was concluded, they could be on their way home to their pedestrian lives. Burnham had managed to have a souvenir program printed. It carried pictures of the track, the happy crowds, the mansions on the Burnham and Grobgy estates, photos of the jockeys in their resplendent raiment, but, of course, no pictures of ponygirls. These were never allowed. Each attendee was searched thoroughly to ensure that no cameras were present. Cell phones were banned in the country so there was no problem in that regard.

The program did contain a brief history of the two ponies, their records and some accounts of their most famous races, all loosely disguised as if they were real ponies. The last page carried some discount coupons that were redeemable at the various merchant tents only after the race.

Jake had awoken early in spite of some three hours of coital madness with Tanya. She had indeed shown him some interesting tricks. Dr. Kevsky had donated a thimbleful of her special tonic so that Jake's stamina would last as long as his desires.

Tanya broke out into tears just before they separated. "I get the feeling that I'm never going to see you again, Jake," she said.

When Jake began a half hearted protest, she put her fingers to his lips. "No, Jake, don't answer. I don't want your last words to me to be a lie. If you are going to stay here in Kalikastan, then I will see you again. If not, I will always have good thoughts about you."

Jake felt like his heart was going to break. Someone had once said that life could not be contained, that it defied all borders that people tried to set for it. Here was life jumping out at him with a vengeance. It was ironic that in all his adult years he had never met anyone who he had such a desire for as the sprightly Russian girl, but it was in a context in which his affection was doomed. He would be sorry for many things when he left Kalikastan.

Looking back, if he had known what he knew now, he doubted whether he would ever have advocated the takeover of the slaving operation in New Jersey. Once he had found out that Maddy was a ponygirl in Kalikastan, he would have stopped right there. He guessed that more than two hundred young, innocent, American girls were now serving as slaves in Kalikastan as a result of their slaving operations back in the States. He could have closed the place down and prevented all of this.

And look what happened to Maureen. She was just another victimized fat girl when he and Irving had found her in the cellar of that Georgia barn so many months ago. Because of him, she was transported to Mexico and made into a whore. While there, she was converted into a pig woman and forced to walk around on all fours. It had been so traumatic that, once she was freed at Irving's insistence and brought to Kalikastan as his price for assisting them, she had lost all desire for life as a woman and pleaded to be made into a ponygirl. As a ponygirl, she had been trained to compete in the heavyweight division and had won a gold medal hauling some 400 kilos of load down and back a 100 meter track. She now sported a gold medal all of her own. But wouldn't she have preferred not to have had to gone through the ordeal at all? He could have prevented it.

And all the slave girls he had used, the ones, and there weren't that many, that he had whipped, all of that would be on his conscience forever.

Then there was Klara, the beautiful blond, Dutch slave girl for whom he had developed such affection. He knew that it was not a true relationship. She was, after all, a slave and could not refuse him anything. But she served him with such complete devotion that he had fallen under her spell. She had been stolen from him, something he attributed to that cold, callous enforcer for the Grobgy clan, Anton Drabik. Jake had sworn to kill Drabik if he could. It was another reason to regret leaving Kalikastan: one task left undone.

Jake looked down at his lover, his eyes misting. "I want you to know that everything that you feel for me, I feel for you. I can't tell you anything about what's in my future, only that these few days with you have been among the happiest of my life. I won't say goodbye. Let's just leave our future open. Anything can happen, and, if it's at all possible, I'll be seeing you again."

With that, the couple kissed and then separated. Jake dressed and, without looking back, left the tent.

It was now about 8:30 A.M. and he, Irving and Irkut were meeting with the Rules committee. Part of the scheme to defeat Lightning in the claiming race was the development of a new ponygirl cart. Irving had been brought in with his scientific expertise to produce a new design. He had done that. The new cart, with which Chocolate had been practicing the 3000 meter at every opportunity, was lighter, more efficient and better at distributing the load of a driver than the traditional sulky cart. Tests had shown that it knocked a full ten seconds off Chocolate's time in the 3000 meter on average. Irkut, with his years of experience in ponygirl racing, had assured them that the new cart would pass muster. This was the moment of truth.

Also present, representing the Grobgy faction, was Jake's nemesis, Anton Drabik. He was fuming at the introduction of the new contraption.

"They can't do this!" he yelled. "They can't introduce a new racing cart now! That's not part of the wager!"

Abdaka Missouli, a native Kalikastani, was the President of the Rules Committee. Irving had been showing him some of the innovations and he was duly impressed. One dramatic change is that the seat for the driver had been moved several inches off center to the left. This meant, since the ponies raced counterclockwise, that there would be more traction as the cart was taken around a curve. There were new alloys used in the construction of the supports and the wheels and Irving had designed a special new lubricant and gearing system, just like a ten speed bike, except that it was automatic.

"I have never seen anything like it!" Abdaka said, waiving off Grobgy's killer. "It's remarkable!"

Irving was beaming with pride.

"There's nothing in the Rules against it," Irkut interjected. "There are no limitations on the sulky carts.

The rules specify only that there will be a driver and two wheels. There's no weight limit nor restriction on gears or anything like that. The goal is to put the fastest pony and cart on the track. That's the tradition. And this cart meets it in every way."

"That's bullshit!" Drabik exclaimed. "There's never been a cart with gears before. It's always been assumed that they were illegal. And the weight is an unfair advantage. We don't have access to those materials."

Abdaka stood up straight and looked at Drabik. "Are you telling me that with all the connections that the clans have in all the countries around the globe, and all your financial resources, you don't have access to someone who could design a cart like this? That's just nonsense and you know it."

"Of course we could have, but it's against the Rules!" Drabik countered.

"Irkut's right," Abdaka retorted. "The description of the sulky cart was left deliberately vague just so that the fastest cart possible could be put on the track. Do you remember the carts when the sport was revived? They were clunky, amateurish things compared with what we race with now. If you brought one of the present day carts back to that time, the other estates would have been hooting and hollering like you are now."

This quieted Drabik down for the moment. Abdaka was right on that point.

"The only thing I'm not sure about are the gears. It seems that you are giving the pony an artificial advantage."

"Not so," Irkut replied. "The driver never touches the gears. They are moved solely by the pony's efforts. The faster she goes, the higher the gear ratio goes, just like on a racing bicycle. No one has ever tried to outlaw them. Just the opposite. And it's no different than the lubricant Irving has designed. It becomes less viscous as the gears heat up, easing the motion of the wheel. All lubricants do that, ours just does it better."

There were two other members of the Rules Committee present. Two votes were needed for a ruling. Since it was undoubtedly a new design, two affirmative votes would be needed to allow its use. One of the judges was in Grobgy's pocket. The other not so and, in fact, had been nominated by a rival clan. So Abdaka was the swing vote.

"Okay, I've seen enough. I need to confer with the Committee members. Please give us a moment."

The three men, all dressed in finely tailored tuxedos, as was the tradition, stepped about twenty yards away from the others so that they could speak privately. Drabik and Jake exchanged death looks. Drabik knew all about why Burnham and Jake had come to Kalikastan. He has gotten some good leads from Jake's slave girl, Klara, under severe torture that is. She was still a forlorn prisoner in the basement of the Grobgy mansion. Drabik went to see her every once in a while just to torment her as a symbol of the hated Americans.

He had said nothing about his discovery. Drabik figured that his knowledge would be his ace in the hole if Lightning lost the race. He would blackmail Burnham into giving her back.

The three men argued back and forth for about twenty minutes. Spectators had already started to filter in to the grandstands and some of them had gathered at the rail to admire the strange, new cart. When the arguments were concluded, the Committee walked back over to where the four men were waiting.

Abdaka spoke for the Committee. "We have considered all aspects of the Rules as it pertains to sulky carts and there does not seem to be any explicit rule that would exclude this cart."

At this Jake, Irkut and Irving perked up.

"On the other hand, the Committee needs to consider the traditions of the sport and whether the innovations would do harm to the sport's purity."

Drabik smiled at the other men. He thought that it was in the bag now. It was just what he had been arguing.

"The sulky races were designed," Abdaka went on, "to be a true test of speed. Therefore, unlike the other races, no limitations were placed on the size of the carts or the weight of the drivers. Speed is the essence of the race and its purity is in seeing that the pony receives no artificial assistance."

Jake's heart sank. They were going to ban the cart.

"The Committee has found by two votes to one that this cart does not violate any of the traditions of the sport," Abdaka announced. Jake's heart leapt for joy.

"It is true that there is a gearing mechanism, but as Irkut has pointed out, it is automatic and requires no actions on the part of the driver to initiate a change. It neither requires any conscious act on the part of the pony, something that would be abhorrent to the sport's basic principles. It will, in fact, be good for the sport, increasing the speed of the sulky races, something that is very much within the intent and spirit of the Rules. Therefore, the cart is approved."

Drabik was hopping mad. "What about the wager? No one said that they could use a new cart!"

"As for the wager," Abdaka stated, "the wager was made subject to the existing Rules. We have found that the cart does not violate the Rules. Therefore the cart does not violate the wager. That is all I'm going to say on the subject. Have a good race gentlemen."

The three Rules Committee members went off to finish their breakfast in the clubhouse.

Drabik issued a cold, malevolent stare at the three other men. They were definitely on his list. Especially that traitor, Irkut. How could he throw his lot in with the Americans?

Jake, Irving and Irkut were gleeful. Especially Irkut, whose reputation was at stake. He looked back at Drabik. He wasn't worried. He had his own protectors in the National Commission. Drabik wouldn't dare do anything to him.

As Drabik strode away, steam pouring from his ears, Irkut hooked the cart up to the work pony and began to lead it to Chocolate's camp site.

* * * * * * * * * * * * * *

That morning found another happy camper. Gregor woke up with his very own slave girl bound and gagged at his feet. She was covered with welts and bruises from their get acquainted session last night. He had been right and poor little Angelique did squeal when her titties were squeezed.

Gregor had a new slave girl, his first, and forty thousand zlotskis burning a hole in his pocket. His tent was out in the outer fringes of the public areas. He wanted to show his new possession off and to prove to his associates that he was less than a fuck up than them.

He first stopped at the breakfast tent and bought rounds of brandy and sessions with three of the sluts who worked there for his friends. He stopped at one of the tents and had a 14 carat gold ring placed in Angelica's nose. He stopped at the tattoo tent and arranged for a giant spider to be tattooed on her back with cobwebs all over her breasts, belly and loins. While that work was being done, he went to the metal working tent and had his personal discs designed, two 14 carat discs for her labia with the emblem of a ferocious spider on them and his name.

He was in one of the upscale refreshment tents, drinking a flagon of ale and getting a blow job from one of the expensive whores who worked there when Drabik's men caught up to him.

* * * * * * * * * * * * * *

Lightning was up early. The day had all the aspects of impending doom to her, despite the brightness and warmth. She went through her morning routines in a mesmerized state. As with all champions, though, she quickly turned her whole being towards victory. She imagined herself on the track, her legs pumping, her chest heaving, and the other pony far behind her. She needed to get into the zone where all champions reside. She had done it many times.

Chocolate was no less nervous. She too seemed in a dream while the black skinned slave girl shaved her skull and loins and teased her pussy until she showed signs of arousal. She had had that dream again last night, the one where she was running in a track meet and the track had turned to a thick, viscous mud, trapping her in place. She had awoken with a start, forgetting where she was and what she had become. When she was able to recover reality, if you want to call it that, she had to fight back tears of fear and sorrow. She rued the day she had taken Jake's offer.

What was a million dollars against her freedom? What a stupid mistake she had made!

Then, like Lightning, her instincts took over. She was a fighter, not a loser. She could beat this other pony, she knew it. That was all she had to do and all of her dreams would come true. She brought her mind to a special place, seeking calmness and contentment in her view of the Pacific Ocean that she imagined from her dream house.

Their drivers were nervous too, although Jerzi was somewhat more nervous than his brother Giorgi. Giorgi just stood to lose a race; he stood to lose his life. He had contemplated going over to Giorgi's campsite and pleading with him to throw the race, but he just could not bring himself to do it. They were not twins, Giorgi was his younger brother by two years. He had always been second in line when growing up. Jerzi had the better record as a ponygirl driver with more gold medals to prove it. This would be the first time that they would be matched against each other in a meaningful race. Although it was not a championship race, it might as well as be for all the attention being devoted to it. No, he couldn't ask Giorgi to throw the race. He just couldn't.

Giorgi knew, of course, that his brother had fucked up by creating a situation where his slave girl felt free to place a stone in Lightning's shoe. He knew that if Jerzi lost, his stock would go way down in racing circles and his would go way up. It was not beyond imagining that he could ride both the 1500 meter and the 3000 meter sulkies next spring and win both championships, something that had never been done. That would erase all the feelings of inferiority that he had experienced in the past.

If he had known how much trouble his brother was really in, well, things would probably have been different.

For all their competitiveness, he still loved his brother. He had, if you pardon the expression, looked up to him almost all his life. They shared the same deformity and had both transformed their liabilities into assets. They were known throughout Kalikastan and both had wonderful houses on Lake Novrograd. They spent every ponygirl summer together on the Black Sea. They could afford the prettiest slave girls in the country. Giorgi would have given all that up in a Moscow minute if he had known what danger his brother was in.

* * * * * * * * * * * * * *

The race was set for 12 noon. By 11 a.m., the stands were mostly filled. Slave girls were scurrying back and forth to deliver refreshments to the fans in the box seats and the whores down at the public level were doing box office business on their backs and on their knees. There had never been a race like this in Kalikastan. Not only did it pit fans of one pony against the other, but it pitted those who were tired of the Russian domination of their country against those dead set against American economic hegemony.

The estate flags of Burnham and Grobgy had been set down near the finish line: Grobgy's yellow, rampant wolf on a field of blue, and Burnham's black mastiff on a field of red. The Kalikastani flag flew high over the stands fluttering in the strong, warm breeze, its mailed fist seemingly slamming up and down in emphasis of the importance of this day.

Burnham and Grobgy had been invited to sit in the Commissioner's Booth. Grobgy had brought a little brown haired girl with him, the one he had been using with such enthusiasm the other day. Burnham brought Betty, as she had wished. There was just one thing. In the morning, he had regretted being so liberal in his speech with her. He couldn't take any chances of her spilling the beans to Jake about his plans. So she was wearing a thick, leather gag in her mouth attached to a leather shield that covered her lips and chin. He had padlocked it closed and had the only key. He was taking no chances. If he really needed a blow job that bad, there were other sluts around.

The two men sat in chairs on opposite sides of the Commissioner's chair. A publicity picture had been taken of the two of them shaking hands. Both men burned bitterly at their proximity and contact with the other. Neither man was used to losing, both men had all of their prestige at stake. The winner would have the fastest ponies in Kalikastan, the loser would be considered a sap.

Grobgy was especially pissed about the switch the American had pulled with the new sulky cart. It was just like the Americans to show off their superior technology and wealth. Well they may have the know how and the money, but he had Drabik. Drabik was the best ponygirl trainer around. He had trained Lightning to be a champion and a champion she was, twice. She was also more experienced in the 3000 meter. If she had not been injured, no pony could have touched her in the Tournament. It was just a shame that Drabik had to go. He was getting too big for his britches. Right after the Tournament, he would have the ponygirl trainer taken care of. And then he would have the randy Anya put away for a while, in some convent maybe, so that she could get a little discipline and some fear of him back. She was just like her mother, who he had to take care of many years ago, wild and indifferent to consequences. Well, she would have to learn, or she would suffer her mother's fate.

In the owner's clubhouse Anya sat alone. Well, almost alone. She had her new slave girl with her, a redhead this time. She wasn't going to perform any sexual acts there in public, mind you, the girl was really there as a status symbol and to give any of her father's friends who stopped by some oral delight, out of her presence, of course. Anya had slept, ironically, the sleep of the just. After all, she was merely putting the world right again, that's all. Drabik had no business being enamored with a ponygirl. It was bad for him. He belonged to her and, sooner or later, she knew he father would make him his successor.

Jake and Irkut had settled into Tanya's family's box, even though she wasn't present. To Jake, her absence was like a wound. His preoccupation with her kept him from noticing the knowing, surreptitious looks that Irkut kept giving him.

Jake's tech guy, Irving joined them soon after. He had gone up to Chocolate's camp site to make sure that the new cart was working right and to make some last minute adjustments to the gears. He had a huge chip on his shoulder as to Jake, who he blamed for Maureen's problems. He still couldn't believe that she wanted to remain a ponygirl and had insisted that Jake take her out too when they rescued Maddy and Jackie.

The rest of the boys, Martinez, Curley, Leon and Tucker, were down in the general admission area mixing with the great unwashed. Once the race was over, and if Chocolate was victorious, they were to rush back to the Burnham estate to set the wheels in motion. All except Martinez. He had made arrangements for their flight out via helicopter and would quietly exit the country into nearby Byelorussia where he had leased a chopper big enough to bring them all out. He was an accomplished pilot and would fly under the radar undetected by Kalikastan's primitive air force.

Burnham had arranged for some of the show ponies to make a demonstration for the crowd while they were waiting for the two stars to appear. Last night, he had funded an immense fireworks display for the amusement of the people who had stayed to watch the race. He had become a true impresario and was enjoying every minute of it.

The show ponies formed several lines on the track's grass infield and were going through routines that they had learned over the last couple of days. Jake spotted the lavender hooded ponies that had enchanted him three days ago at the beginning of the Tournament. They had a fragile grace that made him yearn to possess them. They made him think of Tanya, who had stated that she wanted to train her own show ponies for next year. He wished her well with it and wondered where in the world right then were the innocent, dainty, young women who would be kidnapped and brought to Kalikastan to fulfill her desires. They surely had no inkling of their fate. They were living their lives blissfully ignorant of the harsh future that awaited them. Well, so be it. He could not stop them from being taken and, once they were here, there would be nothing he could do to assuage their fates.

Back in the pony encampment two ponies, like toreadors, were getting ready to do battle. Amanda had given Lightning a thorough rubdown, awakening all of her muscles for their tortuous task. The black haired slave girl was as nervous as a kitten. She knew what was at stake for the ponygirl and her master. She had seen how that dreadful man had looked at him. She also knew that if Lightning lost, she would be sent back to the Grobgy mansion to whatever role fate had in store for her. She didn't want that. She wanted to stay with the little man with the magic prick and take care of the ponygirls for him. She had been through a lot since she came to Kalikastan and this was the best job that she had had yet.

She had polished the sulky cart thoroughly, greased its wheels and oiled the harness straps. Everything appeared in order. She brought Lightning over to the cart and backed her up into the traces, affixing the poles to her hips and the straps to her racing harness. The pony was taller than her and she had to stand on a stool to fasten the reins to her bit. When she was done, she leaned over and gave the pony a kiss in the middle of its forehead. "Good luck, Lightning," she said, a tear in her eye. She had never spoken directly to the pony except to give it orders. She just needed to say something to let it know that she was rooting for it. She gave the pony's breasts an affectionate tweak and then stood down, drew away the stool and knelt in the grass awaiting her master.

Jerzi emerged shortly afterwards from his trailer. He looked up to take a look at the beautiful, blue, Kalikastani sky and took a deep breath of air. He wondered whether he would see another morning. Well, in less than an hour he would know. He was dressed in his silken riding gear, quartered blue and gold, his little cap on his head. The whip that he always used when he raced was hanging by the door and he took it from its hook. Stepping down the last step he walked over to the magnificent pony that he had had the privilege to drive. The doctor had been by this morning and taken another look at her foot. He had just shaken his head and bandaged it up. Yesterday, after the race, her boot had been full of blood.

"These men are fools," he thought. If Lightning ruined her foot in this race, she would probably never champion again. So what was the purpose of running her? If the American won, he might win nothing. If Grobgy won, instead of two champion ponies he might only have one, just as he did now. He thought of poor Natasha, his former slave girl who had suffered a terrible retribution for her sin. He regretted how cruelly he had treated her.

Now that the thought of his own death was so strong with him, there were a lot of things he regretted. Being a ponygirl driver was not one of them. He was proud of the victories he had achieved, would do it all over again if he had the chance. The ponies were beautiful animals, graceful and strong, totally obedient and dedicated to their calling. How much better off they were than living the drab lives they would have been condemned to had they not been converted. Where would they have experienced the thrill of victory so sweet or of defeat so bitter? They experienced highs and lows of pleasure and pain beyond their wildest imaginations.

It was the nearness of death that made the ponygirl driver so philosophical. He shook it off. "I've got a race to run," he thought.

He went cursorily through his routine of checking the pony's harness and the straps that connected her to the cart. Everything seemed as it ought. He stood before her, his head just above the level of her waist. He clicked his fingers and pointed to the ground. Obediently, the pony lowered itself to its knees. He ran his strong, gnarled hands over her sumptuous breasts and gave each nipple a little kiss. He then ran his hand over her hooded head.

"Today's the day, eh *Molnya*," he said to her in Russian. He raised his free hand and stuck out his pointer finger.

"One," he announced in English so that the pony would understand. It was the only English word he had ever used with her. He sensed the pony's understanding. "Good," he thought. He signaled for her to rise and then locked the kneeling Amanda's wrists and ankles together. Not that she would go anywhere, but it was a tradition to leave the ponygirl helpers bound and helpless until their masters' return. They would await it anxiously, their mind focused on the race and hopeful for a victory. Amanda had brought out her gag and he affixed it to her head. After giving her cheek an affectionate tap, he climbed up on the sulky seat and snapped the reins. "Gyup!" he spat out.

Giorgi went through a similar routine. His mind was not on life and death, but glory and defeat. It was the chance of a lifetime to dissipate the shadow that his brother had cast over him, to finally come into his own. And there was a huge reward at stake.

Chocolate had found the change in her handler somewhat disconcerting. She had been used to the blond haired girl and was sorry that she was gone. The black skinned girl though, seemed to know what she was about and she had shaved her head and loins today with authority and given her a good, thorough rubdown. Her body felt all tingly and alive. This was the moment that she had been preparing for for five months. She had failed once, when she was in high school, losing the citywide championship by a few hundredths of a second. It would not happen again, she was determined. And she had every confidence that her driver would know just what to do to bring her to victory. He had driven her to several close victories, achieved only because of his skill and experience. She would be attuned to every nuance of the reins, be ready to give her all when he called for it. Her whole life depended on her obedience to his will, she knew that.

The black skinned girl finished securing the pony to the cart and affixing the reins to her bit. She knew how to handle a ponygirl, having been at it for three years, six seasons. She was especially proud of this one though. The happenstance of their shared racial heritage invested her totally in the pony's success. She knew the pony was American, as she was, although she didn't know from where. It just so happened that Shakira had been plucked from the streets of Muncie, a stone's throw from Chicago, Jackie's home. But that closeness of origin was something Shakira would never know.

A she finished tying off the reins, she leaned over to where the pony's ear lay underneath her silken, red and black hood. "You go, girl!" was all she said.

Jackie recognized the Midwestern urbanized twang immediately. She almost laughed. It was, in fact, inspiring to know that someone of her race, someone who really understood, was rooting for her today. All she could do was issue a little snort and give the slave girl a nod of her head.

Giorgi too, paused in front of his pony before he mounted the cart. He ran his hands over her belly, outlining the black and red mastiff tattooed there and along the inside of her strenuous thighs up to her sexual divide. The black girl had been teasing the slit all morning and Chocolate gave a little jump when he touched her there. Giorgi smiled. She was ready all right. Like his brother, he gave each of her breasts a little kiss and then secured the black skinned slave girl. Taking one last look around his camp site, as if seeking reassurance from its familiarity, he jumped on the cart and signaled his pony to go.

* * * * * * * * * * * * * *

The crowd went wild when Chocolate burst out onto the track for her warm-ups. As the challenger, she entered first. Regardless of their favorite, the onlookers, virtually to a man or woman, were seasoned fans of the sport. Why would they otherwise have driven so many miles to see the Tournament if they weren't? So regardless of which pony they favored, they knew that both ponies were finely tuned, almost perfect specimens of their kind. Blue and gold and red and black pennants were waved about by the crowd in celebration of this special moment. They were on sale at 5 zlotskis each.

When Lightning entered the track about twenty seconds later, the crowd roared again. Everyone in the grandstands was on their feet. Even the slave girls stopped in their tracks and watched the fine animal break out into a trot. The excitement was electrifying. Jake had bought a half pint of gin from a vendor, knowing full well how hard it would be to get service from the slave girls and how desperate his nerves would be for a little calming. He took a deep swig and passed the bottle to his companions. Even Irving, almost abstemious when it came to hard liquor, took a shot.

Drabik was in the stands as well. His angry eyes stared out at the pony that had caused him such torment. Every movement of its fine, long legs, every jiggle of its heavy, lust inspiring breasts sent a tremor through him. He had to have her, even if only to destroy her. The face that he should not have known, the one in the picture that his agents had secured for him, needed to be blotted out forever. He wished that he had never seen it, never seen the pony, never fucked it or placed his hot lips on its teats. But no one could roll back the clock, not even him. He just had to bide his time and hope that he would be granted the chance to expiate his torment.

Both ponies took three turns around the track. The first a slow, warm up lap, the second about at half speed to get all the knots worked out, and the third at a brisk walk. The official with the starting gun took his place. Chocolate stepped up to the starting line first and placed her right foot forward, digging it deeply into the dirt. Her left leg was still sore. The lady doctor had looked at it last night, proscribed some 'relaxation' and then wrapped the leg up tightly. The black girl had rewrapped it this morning after her rubdown as the doctor had shown her. Chocolate could feel its weakness.

Once Lightning took her place in the outer lane, as befitted the 3000 meter champion, the crowd went silent. Both ponies had knots of fear in their bellies. Chocolate, looking sideways at the light skinned pony, wished that she could somehow tell her to let her win the race so that they could both be saved.

Lightning returned the sidelong gaze of the brown skinned pony and felt a tremor of fear. Did the brown pony want to win as badly as she? How could she? No one could have more at stake than her.

It was as if the entire universe was holding its breath. Then, the official pulled the trigger. The noise of the shot echoed over the Kalikastani plain. Within a millisecond, the ponies were off.

Both Jerzi and Giorgi had thought deeply about what strategy to bring to the race and what strategy would likely be adopted by the other. They had both come to the same conclusion. This race would not be won so much by strategy, as by the heart of the ponies they drove. There was no alternative but to go almost wire to wire as fast as they could go. This certainly favored Lightning, since she was much more used to the distance. On the other hand, Chocolate had trained long and hard, something that Jerzi suspected but did not know for sure, and had shown herself quite capable of maintaining a championship pace for the full 3000 meters.

That is not to say that the ponies did not have to be paced properly. It just meant that neither pony could let the other get and maintain the lead for long.

Chocolate was a faster starter than Lightning, and jumped out to an early lead. Jerzi did not want to give the other pony any encouragement, and so a little after the first turn he overtook her. That was fine with Giorgi for now. He would run at the other pony's shoulder for a while to see how its foot was holding up. If he detected any weakness, he would ride it into the ground.

The ponies' only thoughts were about lifting their thighs as high as they could go and getting the best traction that their ponygirl boots would allow. Neither was winded by the ¾ pole.

The ponies crossed the start line after the first lap almost neck and neck. Sweat was pouring down their bodies and the fans at the rail could hear their high pitched grunts and groans as they strained for speed. There was only one man in the crowd that day with a camera. He was the official track photographer. He had been positioned perfectly to catch the two fine, fit ponies as they advanced into their second lap. The color shot he took has a place of honor even today in the owners' clubhouse. In it, you can see the straining leg muscles of both ponies. Chocolate's lips are stretched back in a grotesque grimace, while Lightning seems to be holding her mouth open as far as she could to maximize the air in her lungs. The resolution of the shot is so good, you can see the gleaming of the sweat on their almost perfect bodies. Both pony's ample breasts and long, full ponytails are akimbo and the golden discs in their loins are twinkling in the midday Kalikastani sun. There are, of course, no copies.

Everyone in the crowd wondered when Giorgi would make his move. The race was his pony's to win and Lightning's to lose. He would have to mount a challenge. Jerzi had expected that he would wait until the midpole of the second lap to try and take control of the race. Giorgi surprised him. Just after the ¼ pole of the second lap, he signaled Chocolate to go into full gear.

Jerzi cursed himself for a fool as Chocolate jumped ahead. He gave Lightning the signal to speed up and catch her. For a few seconds, though, the pony hesitated.

For the last five minutes, Lightning had been experiencing exquisite pain in her foot. Each step had become agonizing. She tried to think it away and let the adrenaline of her efforts overcome it. But when he driver signaled her to go faster, she was just landing her injured foot. She tried to use it to push off to accelerate, but a chilling pain shot up her leg and she had to hop to mitigate it. She placed her right foot down and shoved off with that one, but when her injured foot came down again, she had to favor it once more.

Jerzi felt the pony's hesitation. He was ready for it. He reared his whip back and gave her a solid 'crack!' on her back. Lightning's body reverberated at the blow. It was just what she needed. Her mind blocked out the pain in her foot and she planted her left foot down hard and pushed off. Unconsciously, she gave out a weird sounding scream.

Chocolate had gained almost a full length on the pale skinned pony. Everyone in the stands was on their feet. The shouts and yells were deafening. They all knew that they were witnessing greatness and that those fools who had chosen not to stay at the Tournament just one more day would regret it for the rest of their lives.

By the ¾ pole, it looked like Chocolate would win the race. Lightning was not losing ground, but she was not making any up either. Drabik felt his heart in his throat. "No! No! No!" he yelled at the top of his lungs. Grobgy cursed that fucking Jerzi and his whore of a slave girl. He only wished he had her to torment into hell once more. Burnham looked over at the gangster and smiled smugly. He received back an evil sneer.

Jake and his companions were ecstatic. Chocolate was doing it! Everything was breaking as it should! It was too good to believe!

Well, it was too good to believe. Suddenly, Chocolate seemed to slow. Not much, but perceptively to the practiced eye.

"Oh, shit!" Irkut exclaimed, peering at the pony through his binoculars.

"What?" Jake asked, panicked.

"Her leg, she's re-injured it!"

As the ponies started on the home stretch everyone in the stands could see it. Slowly, but surely, Lightning was closing the gap.

Chocolate cursed the world, cursed the driver who had injured her, cursed everything she knew. Her leg felt like someone was driving a spike into it. But she knew that she couldn't stop. She had to keep pounding her feet into the turf. She couldn't help giving just that little preference for her damaged leg and that was making all the difference.

Lightning had been disheartened when she saw that she was doomed. The brown skinned pony's slight reduction in speed gave her hope. "Arrrrrrrrrrgh!" she yelled through her gag and she pushed herself to even greater effort. If only there was enough distance and time, she knew that she could catch her! She knew it!

Jerzi was going wild, cracking his whip and yelling encouragement to his pony. Giorgi was doing the same. Their faces were strained and red, making them look like two demons astride hounds from hell.

Chocolate saw Lightning creeping up to her right. It was her turn to grunt and reach down for her ultimate effort.

They were 300 meters from the finish, 200, 100, 50. Lightning had pulled even and was beginning to surge ahead. 25 meters to go and it looked like it was Lightning's race. The crowd was exploding with fevered screams and yells.

Suddenly, Lightning gave a little jerk forward and stumbled. It slowed her down almost imperceptibly. She lost her stride.

Anya had been waiting all race for something to happen. She had been cursing that fucking Gregor. But now his efforts were bearing fruit.

An experienced slave ponygirl attendant might have seen it. Amanda was not an experienced ponygirl attendant. If Jerzi had not been so preoccupied with issues of life and death, he might have made the inspection that would have revealed it, but maybe not.

Gregor had done this before. Several times. He knew exactly what he was doing. After he left Anya's tent, he took a stroll amongst the ponygirl encampment using the pass that she had given him. Some of the ponies were gone and it was an easy thing to do to slip into one of the abandoned campsites and hide. Security would be tight for anyone entering the pony campground later that night, but there were so many camp sites that no one would be inspecting them one by one.

Later that night, when almost everyone except the most serious revelers had gone to bed, Gregor crept out and made his way silently to Lightning's camp. Drabik had posted a guard, but Gregor slipped his notice easily.

Of the five connections to the pony from the cart, at the shoulders, the hips and in the middle of the back, the one at the middle of its back is the most important. It's the thickest and carries the most strain. It was a simple thing to do to take a rough edged knife and tear at it until it was holding by a slender thread. He poured some brownish dye into the cut. This way, on inspection after the race, the tear would seem to have occurred naturally. Gregor then smeared some brown colored polish on it, the same color as the strap, and covered it with a layer of gloss. When the slave girl went over it, it would look like it didn't need polishing and she would make a cursory pass at it. Only the most practiced eye would have detected it. Amanda's was not such an eye.

Drabik's men had taken Gregor to one of the security tents at the outer edge of the campgrounds. Everyone knew what a slime Gregor was and just the fact of him flashing around money was enough to raise a suspicion that he was up to something. At first, they had tried to weasel it out of him, joking about his good fortune and giving him drinks. But Gregor was an experienced nee'r-do-well. A little liquor wasn't going to get him to put himself in the soup. After a little while, the boys began to get rough. But Gregor, although a dullard and a lowlife, was a tough motherfucker. It took a good two hours to get him to talk. Unfortunately, the race had just gone off and it was too late to warn Drabik so that he could stop it. It was also unfortunate that Gregor was so tough because the same extreme measures that got him to talk brought about his expiration. He was as dead as a doornail, something Angelique would later be very happy to learn but, unfortunately, too late to avoid being tattooed like a circus freak, and his testimony would never be able to be brought in front of the Racing Commission. Anya, in spite of herself, had pulled it off.

Lightning tried desperately to regain her balance. She could not understand what had happened. Jerzi saw the strap part and he cursed heaven for his foolishness in not checking it better. All Chocolate knew was that Lightning had dropped back a step. Three agonizing steps later, she crossed the finish line first.

CHAPTER SIX

A wave of fear, loneliness, heartache and devastation passed through Lightning as she realized that she had failed. Her legs collapsed underneath her and she tumbled down to the ground. The velocity of the cart behind her pushed her body firmly into the dirt of the track. She was out of breath, but between her desperate gasps for air, she began to sob uncontrollably.

The crowd, which had been ebullient at Chocolate's victory and the excitement of the race, uttered a great moan as they saw the fine ponygirl go down. From the stands, it was not clear what had caused her collapse.

Up in the clubhouse, Anton Drabik just stared out at the body of the ponygirl, squirming in the dirt, and burned. He, who had witnessed a thousand ponygirl races, knew exactly what had happened. It was just then that one of his men who had been dealing with Gregor came rushing in. He showed Drabik a written account of what Gregor had told his men. Drabik crushed the note in his hand. People were going to pay, that was for sure.

Jake, Irkut and Irving went wild as they saw Chocolate begin her victory lap. For a moment, none of them noticed that Lightning had fallen. When they did, silence fell over them. Irkut's eyes had been peeled on Chocolate and her aggravation of her leg injury and had not seen the cause of Lightning's misstep. He knew immediately that his place was down on the track. If Lightning now belonged to Mr. Burnham, then she was his responsibility.

"Come on, Jake," he said. We've got to get down there!"

Jake gave a knowing look at Irving. Irving nodded. The plan had to be set in motion.

Chocolate was overwhelmed with relief, happiness, pride. She too knew nothing about the equipment malfunction. At this point, she didn't care what caused her to win. She knew only that the process by which she would be brought home was now started. She had done her job!

Giorgi was also overcome with elation. He had done it! He had beaten his brother! He would get a big reward from the American billionaire and the accolades of all of his confreres. He eased the ponygirl into a trot and began his victory lap. He was surprised that he did not hear more noise from the crowd. He was the man of the hour wasn't he? Chocolate had shown herself to be among the best ponygirls of all time, hadn't she? Why was the crowd so quiet? When he came around the far turn and got a view of the finish line and the small crowd of officials surrounding the ponygirl in the dirt, he knew why. What had happened? He rushed his limping pony up to where the small group was standing and he hopped off his cart.

Jerzi was standing next to his cart. If Lightning was disconsolate, he was crushed. It was a sentence of death, he knew it. He glanced up at the clubhouse and although he couldn't see the dark eyed killer, he knew that the man was watching him. Giorgi came running up as fast as his feet could carry him.

"What's the matter?" he shouted.

Jerzi, his racing cap in his hand merely gestured down at the sobbing ponygirl.

The track physician had run out as well as several of the officials. A small crowd was assembling around the distraught pony.

Suddenly, the officials and the doctor were pushed aside. It was Nicholai Borodin, Burnham's chief of security, and several of his men. Two of the men began to unhook the ponygirl from the cart. Two others made a small cordon around her. The message was clear: Lightning belonged to Michael Burnham now.

When Irkut and Jake arrived, the men were lifting the pony to her feet. She was like a mass of jelly, limp as a dish rag. Her chest was heaving from her sobs. Although Irkut insisted to be allowed to examine her foot, the security men held him and Jake off.

"Burnham's orders," was all that Borodin would say.

Burnham was on his way down. He was overcome with glee at his success. He had given a nod to Grobgy, who, if looks could kill, would have had Burnham skewered and roasted alive. Then he had dashed down towards the track.

One of the track officials motioned for Giorgi to bring Chocolate into the winner's circle. Obediently, and to claim his moment of glory, Giorgi hopped back on the sulky seat and directed his pony towards the gate that led there.

Once Lightning had been brought to her feet, the crowd, assuming that she was all right, again began to cheer and shout in favor of the victor. "*Scho-ko-lad-niy! Sho-ko-lad-niy! Scho-ko-lad-niy!*" they began to chant rhythmically. As Chocolate pulled into the winner's circle, the noise became deafening.

Burnham arrived at the same time. Giorgi jumped down from his perch and they gave each other hearty handshakes. A large garland of flowers was placed around Chocolate's neck by someone. Someone else handed

Burnham a magnum of champagne. The track photographer took a picture of the three of them, Chocolate, Giorgi and Burnham. Then Borodin's men dragged Lightning into the ring. Jake and Irkut followed. The men pulled Lightning over to where Chocolate stood and, with the men holding Lightning up by the arms, another picture was taken. A third picture, the one most often referred to later, included the Ponygirl Racing Commission President, Irkut, Burnham, Chocolate and Lightning, with the security men standing discretely behind her.

As soon as the picture was taken, Burnham signaled Borodin and he and his men began to hustle the ponygirl away. A ponygirl trailer had been brought up. The men pulled the pony into it, fastened her in place, and the trailer was driven off.

Irkut protested. "Her foot!" he yelled at Burnham over the crowd noise. "Someone's got to look at her foot!"

Burnham waved him off. "Don't worry. She'll be taken care of," was all he said. Basking in his victory, he raised the champagne bottle to his lips and took a large swig.

The ebullient billionaire had dragged Betty down to the winner's circle with him. One of the security men had been holding the leash that connected to her large, golden nose ring while Burnham had been having his picture taken. He now handed it back.

Betty saw Jake standing there like he was an abandoned child. Burnham's seizure of the pony had been swift, efficient and decisive. It did not bode well for their plans to rescue her. She tried and tried to get Jake's attention. She had to talk to him! She just had to! Maybe later, on the ride back to Burnham's estate she could tell him what she knew, but he would have to make a point of taking her out of her cage and bringing her into his room. Even with the gag on, she could still write with her hands, somehow make Jake understand her. But he had to know that she needed to speak with him or he might ignore her.

Jake saw the frantic eyes of the bird woman. He put it down to her trying to remind him of his promise. He remembered it well. He would do the best that he could. He was not going to jeopardize the whole Maddy and Jackie rescue.

A huge crowd had surrounded the victorious pony and Chocolate was beginning to panic. Strange hands rubbed her body, her breasts, her rear, her thighs. People's bodies were being pressed against her. Giorgi saw what was happening. He signaled to the track security men and they formed a wedge to help him get back to his cart and then to create a space between Chocolate and the crowd. When he gained the room, Giorgi carefully backed the pony from the ring and took her back out onto the track.

He couldn't resist it and, as a matter of fact, the crowd would have been disappointed if he hadn't done it. He took Chocolate on another victory lap. This time, the crowd did cheer. He waved his cap with one hand while holding on to the pony's reins with the other. People were waving their Burnham pennants exuberantly while others were throwing their Grobgy pennants on to the track. When Chocolate came around the home turn and began to pass in front of the grand stands once again, Giorgi brought her to a canter, and, high stepping past the delirious fans, trampled the Grobgy pennants beneath her feet.

Upstairs, Grobgy was watching. A pit had opened up in his stomach. Dynasties had fallen for less. He knew that his stock had gone way down this day. He needed to get back to his estate as soon as possible and make sure that his empire did not crumble. The first thing that he would do, once there, would be to arrange for Drabik's execution.

Drabik also sensed the dramatic lessening of Grobgy's prestige. This would make his job all the easier. Any of his lieutenants and co-conspirators who were wavering would be buttressed now. That was the good part. The bad part was watching the focus of all of his lusts and desires being carted away. He had a plan to recover her. Burnham wouldn't dare keep her once he revealed what he knew. Even if the National Commission didn't take action against him, their confidence in him would ebb. He knew that Burnham, with all of his fancy plans, could not afford that.

Before he went back to the Grobgy estate to put his schemes into motion, however, there was something that he had to do.

* * * * * * * * * * * * *

Giorgi drove Chocolate through the congratulatory throng that lined the service road in the ponypark. He was looking forwards to a celebratory fuck of the delightful pony and then, from a regal perch, doling out her favors to his friends. Chocolate, too, was looking forwards to finally being able to stuff a cock up her holes. She had experienced a long series of manually encouraged orgasm ever since she had been hurt, but had been denied the use of a good, thick prick.

They were both to be disappointed. When the flower festooned pony and her driver reached the campsite, they were surprised to see that it had been cordoned off by Borodin's security men. It was like an armed camp. Giorgi was permitted to drive the cart into the clearing, but when he hopped off and started forwards to release the pony from her bindings, he was pushed aside.

"We'll do that," a beefy, rough looking man said. He was dressed like all of Borodin's security team in a black t-shirt with the signature black mastiff of Burnham's emblem outlined in red over the left part of their chest, a pair of black dungarees and shiny, black combat boots. The other men were carrying M-16's, locked and loaded, but this man, apparently their leader, sported a Glock 9 millimeter on his hip.

"What the fuck's going on?" Giorgi protested. Of course, it's hard to project an aura of forceful outrage when you're only 4'2" tall.

The team leader had an envelope for Giorgi. He handed it to him. It was his bonus check from Burnham, 1,500,000 zlotskis, about $325,000.

"What the fuck is this?" Giorgi asked. It was a profound breach of protocol not to let the ponygirl driver celebrate with the ponygirl on the day of an important victory, and this was among the most important there ever was.

"Mr. Burnham sends his thanks. We're taking possession of the pony. That's all there is to it. If you have a problem with that, you'll have to take it up with Mr. Burnham."

Chocolate too was affronted by the break from tradition. And more than that, the presence of so many security men did not bode well for Jake's efforts to rescue her. A pit of fear opened up in her belly.

She did not have long to contemplate this new development. Once the men had unhooked her from the sulky cart, one of them attached a leash to her nose ring. A ponygirl trailer was pulled into the camp area towed by a small pickup truck. Black, of course, with Burnham's logo on its side.

Unceremoniously, the pony was dragged into the trailer. Her nose ring was affixed to a ring in the wall at the front of the trailer and her belly was forced up against the thick rail that ran across it. In a trice she was secured to it and her ponygirl boots were locked into rings on the floor, spreading her legs about three feet apart. The men hopped out of the trailer, the engine gave a little roar and she was on the move.

Helpless, Giorgi watched his ponygirl being hauled away.

* * * * * * * * * * * * * * *

Jerzi had caught a ride with one of the carts hauled by two workponies back to his campsite. All the way back, he was morosely considering his options. He could run. But where would he go? He would have to hide out like a fugitive from justice which, in a way, he was. He knew, though, that Drabik and his men would pursue him like furies from hell. He cursed himself for not examining Lightning's rig more carefully, cursed himself for his foolishness in letting his slave girl, Natasha, torment the pony to begin with.

No, the only option was to stay and accept whatever Drabik meted out. There was always the chance that he would decide to let him live, although that chance was slim. Drabik was not known as a man who made empty threats.

When they arrived at his campsite, he hopped off the cart and thanked the driver. Amanda was kneeling there waiting for him and he could see the unhappiness in her eyes as she recognized immediately how the race had gone.

They welled up with tears and she gave a low moan, all the expression that her thick gag permitted her.

She turned on her knees as he walked by her. He was not in the mood to unfasten her yet. What was the point? He was certainly not going to fuck her and there was nothing he needed now except a full glass of vodka.

Tossing his blue and gold cap onto the ground, Jerzi stepped into his trailer and emerged with a liter of vodka and a glass. His chair was where it always was and he sat down in it and poured himself a hefty shot. He downed it instantly and then poured himself another.

A feeling of sorrow came over him, sorrow that it all had to end this way. But, he had had a good run. He had ridden to glory many times, just yesterday in fact. He had driven and fucked the best ponygirls in the country. He had had plentiful access to bevies of beautiful slave girls over the years, some granted as boons for his victories by grateful owners, some purchased by him for his amusement.

He would miss his brother, Giorgi. He had proven himself the best ponygirl driver around. Were it not for the break in the strap, maybe he would have won, but that was not certain. Chocolate had a lot of heart and who knows, she might have, at Giorgi's urging, been able to summon up one last gargantuan burst of speed and overcome Lightning's surge. He had to admire Giorgi's strategy. His breakout at the ¼ pole of the second lap had been a stroke of genius. He knew that he had it in him.

Jerzi poured himself another shot and gulped it down. He looked over at the forlorn, black haired slave girl. She had taken some work, but all in all she had proven a good servant. She loved to fuck and she was good with the pony.

At that moment a thought occurred to him. Drabik was a vindictive bastard. If Amanda had been more scrupulous in her duties, or, to be fair, more experienced, she might have caught the sabotage to the middle strap. Drabik would certainly see it that way. Natasha had suffered a horrible fate for what she had done. Would the callous killer take vengeance out on the slave girl as well?

He rose from his chair and stepped over to where Amanda was kneeling in the grass. He unhooked her bound wrists from her ankles and freed her legs.

"Stand up," he ordered her in English.

The slave girl rose slowly. He could see that she was trembling. Her full sized breasts were quivering. It touched him that she had such concern for him. Or, maybe she realized as well as he did the danger she was in. She knew nothing about how he had lost the race, only that it had, in fact, been lost. She had seen Drabik throwing his weight around the campsite and certainly had taken in the ominous threats he had made, even if they were in Russian.

No matter. He couldn't allow her to be punished for what were essentially his sins.

"I want you to go down to the food station where you pick up my meals," he told her. "I want you to wait there. Do not on any account come back to the campsite. Do you hear me?"

Amanda, her eyes full of tears, shook her head 'no'. She didn't want to leave the little man. He was the best master she had ever had. Probably the best she ever would. What was the sense of going on as a slave girl anyway? What kind of life would she have?

Jerzi looked at her sternly. She was short, but he was even shorter. Nonetheless he seemed to loom over her. "Don't spoil everything by being disobedient now," he told her. "You are a slave girl. A slave girl obeys without question. I don't know why fate brought you here to

Kalikastan, but it is not up to you to decide what happens to you. Whatever the fates cast your way after today, you must accept it. Do you understand, or do I have to whip you?"

Whipping her was the last thing that he wanted to do now, but if he had to to make her go, he would do it.

Tearfully, Amanda shook her head 'no'. She stepped forward and pressed her body against the little man to feel the warmth and magic of his body one last time. Then she turned and ran.

* * * * * * * * * * * * * *

To say that Lightning was disconsolate would be like saying that the ocean has water in it. Her desolation filled her whole being. When the men lifted her up from the ground after the race, she wanted to fight them off, but was incapable of any volitional movement. What happened next was just a blur. She remembered standing somewhere for as few moments with a crowd of people around and then being hustled off into a ponyvan. She wanted to collapse to the floor, but the men tied off her nose ring to the wall in front of her and then buckled her waist to the cross bar. Once they had her boots fastened to rings in the floor, the van moved off.

It was a short ride, but she was left inside the van for a long time. She was used to standing silent and motionless for long periods, but the sorrow which had pierced her very being had destroyed all of her equanimity. Not since she had first been dehumanized had she felt so her lack of power over herself and the things around her. She had lost her master, probably forever. Why the strap broke at her back, she didn't know. Was it God's hand reaching down to force her to expiate some sin that she did not know she had committed? Did God's writ run to this strange land she was in, or had the devil taken sole possession of the place? How could such a place exist? How could people, thousands of them, live with themselves for fostering and supporting a system which destroyed other people's very humanity? Why was all this happening to her?

She thought of the hot hands of her now former master, how he had driven her to pleasure many times and how she had reveled in it. His gesture last night proved that he loved her, didn't it? He had brought her misery too, it's true. He had been the one who deprived her of her womanhood. He had whipped her mercilessly many times. But if it had not been him, it would have been somebody else. He made her a champion, forced her to draw inside her and tap the well of strength that she had not even known was there.

Now she would be the prisoner of others. Who would love her? Who would see the last spark of humanity in her? It was like losing her personhood all over again. These new men would fuck her, fill her mouth with their cocks, lock her away in their barn and whip her for their amusement and when she committed any of a host of minor faults.

But then, she had a choice didn't she. She had the choice that all ponygirls had. She could choose to reject the men's authority over her, their ability to make her run, suck their cocks, open herself willingly to them. She would suffer, yes, suffer unto death. But that was a choice she could make.

A giant sob seized her body and it shook as if it was in the midst of an epileptic fit. As she moved the small amount that her confinements permitted her, she heard her two championship medals clink together under her chin.

She had always thought of her championship medal with pride. It set her apart from the other ponygirls, ensured that she was not entirely deprived of personality. It had become, instead, a symbol of her cowardice. She was afraid to challenge the men, afraid of the exquisite pain they could bring her, afraid to deny them her whole being. She had not just accepted her role as a ponygirl, she had become the apotheosis of ponygirldom.

Lightning had no idea how long it was before they came to took her out of the van. It seemed longer than it was because of her distraught state. It was actually only about 45 minutes.

Burnham's staff doctor was supposed to meet them at this camp site that Borodin's men had secured, but he didn't show. He was needed to see to the pony's injury. Borodin's men scoured the encampments to try and find him. The looked in the various entertainment tents, the tents of the traveling whorehouses, everywhere. Everywhere except in his own tent. He had passed out there at about 6 a.m. that morning after a night long revelry. The slave girl that he had brought back to his tent was kneeling by his side, her arms bound behind her and wearing a gag. She was clearly in distress since she had been kneeling this way since well before 6 a.m. when the doctor finally surrendered to the idea that he had consumed too much alcohol to perform and, instead, passed out. She had to pee like a racehorse.

When it finally occurred to them to look there, four men converged on his tent. Two of Borodin's men dragged him to his feet and shook him until he came to consciousness.

"Wha...?" he mumbled.

"You have a patient, doctor," one of the men said, placing a deliberate, ironic emphasis on the word 'doctor'.

"Oh, oh, yes, the ponygirl," he answered. "How long until the race?" he asked.

The men all laughed. The man who spoke earlier told him, "The race has been over for almost an hour, doctor. She's waiting for you, and by now, the other one too."

"Oh, gosh," the doctor mumbled. "You had better take me to them. But first," he said, looking down at the half empty bottle of vodka on the floor of the tent, "I need a little hair of the dog. You boys don't mind, do you?"

"Sure we mind," the apparent leader of the group said. "Let's go take care of the ponygirls first, then you can drink all you like."

One of the men was left behind to make sure that the slave girl got relief and that she was returned to her owner, whoever that was. A tall, brown haired man, was given the assignment. He leashed the slave girl and then brought her out of the tent. He signaled her to crouch down on the grass and let it flow. During the encampment, there were, necessarily, latrines and portable johns for things like this, but everybody was leaving today and so, what difference did it make? When she was done, he led her back into the tent and told her to resume her kneeling position. He lowered his zipper. She needed no instruction on what to do next. No sense wasting a perfectly good slave girl.

When the doctor arrived at the campsite where Lightning was being held, she was taken from her trailer so that he could look at her foot. The man who unhooked her gave her pussy a good rub before her brought her out. Lightning tried to fight off the sensations of arousal, but it had been so long and just this morning the black haired girl had teased her slit to near completion several times. She cursed herself and her need. The man just laughed at her easily produced signs of lust.

The unhappy pony was forced to lie on her back while one of the men removed her boot. It was, like yesterday, full of blood.

Lightning had been unconscious of how much her injury was hurting her, but now that the boot was off, it hit her like a punch. She was still wearing her racing bit and her teeth clamped down on it while she issued a piteous moan.

The doctor was taken aback. "This must really hurt," he said to no one in particular.

"No shit," one of the security men said to him.

Fortunately, one of the security men had retrieved the doctor's bag and he immediately gave her a shot for the pain. He cleaned out the wound and bandaged it back up.

"No standing for this pony," he announced. "The foot should be elevated to cut down on the swelling."

Borodin had taken over the duties of caring for the two champion ponygirls. He had already arranged it so that the pony could be strapped lying down in the ponytrailer on the way back to the estate.

"This may need surgery," the doctor opined as he finished wrapping the foot.

"Not by you," Borodin answered him.

Lightning was permitted to lie in the grass while the men removed Chocolate from her trailer. She too had been standing for a long time. She, however, had been fully conscious of the pain emanating from her leg the whole time. Tears were flowing from her shrouded eyes as she begged silently for someone to come and get her off of her feet. When she was brought out of the trailer, she collapsed to the ground.

"Oh, my," the doctor said. He immediately gave Chocolate a shot just like he had given Lightning. He felt the muscle of her thigh and then proceeded to wrap it.

"No standing for this pony either," he stated. "She needs to rest her leg for at least 24 hours before she walks on it again."

Borodin had made provision for that as well.

Once the doctor had finished, a double wide ponygirl trailer was driven into the enclosure. The men lifted the two ponies into it and strapped them down on the floor, ironically, right next to each other. The Velcro flaps over their eyelets were closed, sealing them in darkness. They were barely conscious of what was happening to them. They hardly noticed when the trailer was hauled back onto the service road to begin the 13 hour drive to the Burnham mansion.

* * * * * * * * * * * * * * *

Jake had been impressed with Burnham's *coup de main* in isolating and taking possession of the ponygirls. It put a wrench in his plans. He had fully expected Burnham to spend the rest of the day celebrating and luxuriating in his victory by showing off the two fastest ponygirls on Earth. Martinez was not scheduled to bring in the helicopter until the day after tomorrow. Jake had also been surprised, although he shouldn't have been, at the high level of security that had been applied to the ponygirls. It did not bode well for their rescue operation. It looked like they were going to have to shoot it out with Borodin's security men before getting the girls out. A shootout would be messy and noisy and anything could happen. They had no provision for medical treatment until after the twenty minute helicopter flight to the Byelorussian border. If either of the girls were shot, they could easily die before they even got there.

He had called a meeting of his men before the drive back. Curley, Leon and Tucker were going in one car and he and Irving were going in another.

"Well," he said, "any ideas."

"It looks like we will have to shoot it out," Leon said. Aside from Martinez and Irving, and, of course, Jake, there was not a lot of brain power on Jake's team. Curley, Leon and Tucker had been chosen for their coolness in tight situations and Tucker especially for his brawn.

"What are we going to use," Curley asked, "pop guns?"

"I don't know," Jake answered. I hate the idea of going up against those M-16's with just sidearms."

"You don't have to," Irving interjected.

"What?" Jake shot back.

"I said, you don't have to. While the rest of you have been sitting on your asses or fucking pretty little slave girls, I have been working."

"And?" Jake asked pointedly.

"You're not the only one with ideas, Jake. I knew that something like this would happen. I was telling Martinez just a couple weeks ago,,,,"

"Irving!" Jake shouted. "Get to the point!"

"Well, I'd been working on some tranquillizer rifles back at my lab in Sarasota. We developed a prototype a couple of months back and it tested out okay so I authorized the production of two more."

"Tranquilizer rifles? You mean they shoot darts?" Leon asked.

"Yes, darts." Irving answered. "The rifle can land a dart within a three inch diameter space from a hundred yards.

Each rifle can hold ten rounds. When the projectile strikes the victim, it releases a nerve toxin under their skin. Unconsciousness comes in about 2.2 seconds."

"That's great, Irving," Jake told him. "I hate to rain on your parade, but we're in Kalikastan. It might take a week to get your rifles out here, even assuming that we could get them in past customs. We don't have a week. I think that Burnham's smelled a rat and, unless I mistake my man, he will take us out of the picture long before that."

"You know," Irving shouted, his face brewing up to a fire engine red, "you really piss me off! If it weren't for you, we could have saved Maureen a world of anguish! You let this slaving thing get way out of hand! And now you've fucked up the rescue plan because Burnham is smarter than you. Do you think I would have even mentioned the rifles if they would take a week to get here! Martinez flew them in a week ago. They're in a farmhouse about fifteen miles from the estate. All we need to do is go there and get them!"

"Whoa, Irving! Take it easy," Jake replied. "We can have a debate on whether we achieved a net good or a net bad when we get out of this, and whether I'm smarter than Burnham. For now, let me say that I'm glad that you and Martinez took the initiative. And I'm sorry if I sometimes under appreciate you, Irving. Between us, I think you're the tops."

This last was said with a tone of some amusement. The boys got a laugh out of it. It just made Irving madder.

"This is the last time, Jake…" Irving started to say.

"Irving!" Jake yelled. "Cool down! This is business, remember! You came up with a great idea and it looks like it will help us. Just tell me, how loud are the shots when they go off?"

Irving got control of himself. Jake was right. When the shit got going, the coolest heads usually prevailed.

"It makes a little popping sound. I built a silencer system into them. No one who's more than fifty feet away from you will hear it."

"Okay," Jake replied. "Here's what we'll do."

* * * * * * * * * * * * * *

Michael Burnham was beside himself with delight. He had pulled it off! And he had gotten the jump on Jake, too! Life was just great. It was not so great, though, for the black haired slave girl he had been tormenting with his favorite riding crop.

They were on their way back to his estate in his luxurious trailer. He was in the bedroom of the trailer and the girl was standing in front of the bed, her hands chained to the ceiling. She was already wearing several deep red bruises across her breasts and thighs. She was gagged so that she wouldn't make too much noise. Burnham was naked and sitting on the edge of his bed with his hand in her quim. Despite her lingering pain from his assaults, she was beginning to pant and moan from his efforts.

It was funny when he thought of it. The best thing that had ever happened to him, aside from becoming a billionaire, that is, was having his niece kidnapped. It was a clear case of silver lining and all that crap. If she had never been kidnapped, he would never have called Jake. If he hadn't called Jake, Jake would not have gotten the idea of taking over the slaving operation in New Jersey and bluffing their way into Kalikastan. If he hadn't bluffed his way into Kalikastan, he wouldn't be sitting here now with his hand up the purse of a beautiful, young, girl, a whip in the other and a hard on as big as Texas. Not to mention all the other amenities. He was making a fortune, or rather, another fortune, off of the pipeline. He personally owned about forty slave girls of all types and flavors, he had his own slave training facility, his own ponygirl stable and a bevy of underworld connections that would help extend his reach all over the globe. The US government was under-writing and/or ignoring much of his operations in exchange for secret prison facilities in the country and help with certain antiterrorist 'black ops'. No one on the globe could touch him. The only fly in the ointment was Jake and his boys.

Jake had begged off returning to the estate in his trailer, saying that he wanted to spend some time with his new 'girlfriend' before he went back. Burnham had had her checked out and he knew for a fact that she had left with her father that morning. He had been right. Jake was up to something. He would be ready for him.

Betty, the bird woman, was on all fours on what would have been Jake's bed if he had opted to return with Burnham. There were five of Burnham's security men in the trailer and they had nothing else to do, so she had been fucking them for the last hour or so. The first three had brought her explosive orgasms. Burnham still had the gag locked in her mouth and so she had to satisfy the men with her other two orifices. The man who was fucking her now, the fourth man to fuck her, was sawing in and out of her rear aperture. It was driving her crazy. Every time she came close to an orgasm, he would sense it and stop. When he did, she would give out a deep moan and all the men would laugh.

Betty had real reason to worry. Burnham had told her that the Japanese man who wanted to buy her would be at the estate in a day or so to look over Burnham's slave training facility. There had been talk of building a lab for the man and his lover, a female, American doctor, a surgeon, she understood, where they could continue certain 'experiments'. The man apparently had some ideas that would benefit the slave training regimen as well. She had to get out of Kalikastan or her life would become even more miserable than it was now. She loathed the men who were abusing her. She loathed how they made her come against her wishes and how they received such amusement from it. Most of all, she loathed how Burnham had made her into some strange creature. She imagined the view of her body received by the man who was plowing her ass with such careful skill. Her pale white thighs and ass were presented to him. The rest of her was a kaleidoscope of color.

The man had begun his sawing again. Her little round hole tingled where the fat cock abraded it. The tingling went directly to her mushy canal. Her breasts were hard with her arousal and her whole body felt electrified. This would be her fifth orgasm in the last hour. Sooner or later, she would run out and they would begin beating her. She knew that. But she couldn't help herself.

The fat cock went on and on. She began to huff and puff on the bed as she thrust her hips back to meet each forward thrust of the man behind her. Her hands were balled into fists and her head was pressed down on the soft, cool mattress. Her breasts swayed and jiggled as they recorded each collision of the back of her thighs and the front of her assailant's. It seemed like the man was going to let her crest. He was huffing and puffing himself and his grip on her hips had gotten stronger, more emphatic. The other men in the room began clapping. It was timed to the man's thrusts. Suddenly, the man gave a shout of glee. He reached under Betty's torso and grabbed her breasts and he drove his cock even deeper into her bowels. She could feel his prick as it entered its convulsions. She felt herself go over the top. "Mmmmmmmm! Mmmmmmmmm!" she moaned. The contractions of her womb sent a wave of pleasure through her. "Oh, god! Oh, god!" she thought as it rolled on and on. The man clenched her tits tightly as he pounded his cock into her. The other men all cheered.

When the man had exhausted his forces, he pulled his now limp cock from her ass. She was breathing heavily. Her tiny rear star felt stretched and open. Her pussy burned with the aftereffects of her orgasm. She heard the men passing a bottle of vodka around. There was some arguing, some talking and then, apparently some agreement. She felt the mattress depress behind her. A fat cock poked its bulbous head at the entrance to her bowels and began to slide inside. The tingling in her pussy began again.

* * * * * * * * * * * * * *

It seemed that everyone was leaving. Grobgy and Drabik had left. The entertainment tents had been folded up. A line of men was scouring the camp grounds picking up the garbage and litter of four days of partying. Poor Amanda was still sitting on the steps of the food hut waiting for someone to come and get her. It had been hours since the little man had sent her away.

Naked and bound, there was not much more Amanda could do than wait. Her only alternative was to go back to the campsite and see if the coast was clear. Maybe the dark visaged man had not hurt the little man too badly. Maybe he was lying there in need of medical attention! Maybe it was okay to go back.

She was tired, frightened, lonely, hungry, thirsty. She had to do something. Finally, she mustered the courage to go back to the campsite. She planned to sneak up on it so that maybe if the bad man was still there he wouldn't see her.

Things had changed since Amanda had fled the camp site. Most of the ponies had been packed up and the trailers driven away. She remembered that she had to turn right at the blue trailer and then left at the red one. But the blue trailer was gone and the red one too. Which way should she go?

What should have taken about five minutes took the unhappy slave girl almost an hour. Eventually, she recognized, from afar, the trailer that belonged to the little man. All of the trailers that had been near it were gone and there was no way she could sneak up on it. There didn't seem to be anyone there, though and so she chanced it.

At first, she didn't see anything. The pony wasn't there, but she knew that she would not be. The fire was still burning slightly and a circle of smoke was wafting up from it. The little man's whips still hung from the nail next to the trailer door. She would be pissed if he went off drinking with some of his buddies, the ones that he made her fuck, and left her to stew down at the food hut.

Then she saw it. It looked like a little bundle of ragged clothing, only it was shiny and blue and gold, just like the little man's racing uniform. She crept closer. She saw a boot, then two. It was the little man. He was lying face down in the grass. As she came closer she saw that he was dead. There was a hole in the back of his head and blood had flowed out everywhere. She imagined that the dark man had made her master kneel down and look away from him before he shot him.

Amanda started to cry. She quickly looked around to see if the dark man was anywhere about. She didn't see him. She looked back at the only master she had had who had really meant something to her. He was dead and would never fuck her again. She became overwhelmed with sorrow. It was too much to take. She spun around and ran back the way she had come.

It was a little after sundown. The sky was getting dark although there was till a little twilight left. Amanda had wandered around for hours. She didn't know what to do or where to go. She had heard that they did terrible things to slave girls who ran away and she didn't want anyone to think that she was doing that. But what was to become of her? She couldn't free her hands or remove her gag. It would be cold soon and she was as naked as the day she was born. The men who were cleaning up paid no attention to her other than to call out to her once in a while in Russian, undoubtedly something coarse and salacious. When they did that, she ran away.

She was sitting by the side of one of the service roads, she didn't know which one. She was crying again. It seemed that she had spent most of the day crying. She had long ago become acclimated to the fact that she was a slave girl now and never would be anything else. But why did all these things keep happening? Why couldn't she just get one master and please him? Why did everything bad seem to happen to her?

Just then a pickup that had been working its way down the service road slid to a stop. It was pulling a large trailer and had a large, folded up tent, in its bed. A youngish man, maybe about thirty, with a scruffy, black beard, rolled down the window and took a look at her. He said something to someone who was sitting next to him and then she heard the door of the pickup opening on the other side. She saw a man circling around the back of the trailer. By the time that she decided that it would be better if she ran away, the other man was out too.

"What have we here?" he said jovially. "Lost?"

Amanda just shook her head. She wasn't lost, not really. And she didn't like the looks of these guys.

The first man had finished his circumnavigation of the trailer and was walking up to her. He looked older than the driver, maybe 45 or even older. He was clean shaven and was wearing a dirty t-shirt and jeans, just like the first man. He stood in front of her.

"Stand up, cunt," he said sharply.

Amanda sprung to her feet. She didn't like the sound of this.

The men looked at her naked body, her large, jutting breasts, her curvaceous hips, her pleasantly formed thighs. They said something to each other in Russian. There was a little debate. Then the first man, the coarse one, addressed her again.

"Turn around, slut," he said. The men took a good look at her ass. She felt hands assessing its firmness.

"Now back again," he barked.

Fearfully, Amanda obeyed. She was trembling now. Something was going to happen, she just knew it.

The first man grabbed hold of her breasts and squeezed them hard. She gave out a little squeal of pain. The men both laughed. "Turn around and bend over," the second man said. "And spread your legs."

There was not a chance in hell that Amanda would disobey them, even though she wanted to with all her soul. Her heart was pounding in her chest. The trailer behind the pickup loomed like some house of horrors. Whatever was back there, she didn't want to know.

She turned, obediently, and bent over as far as she could without falling over. She spread her legs in compliance with the man's demand and to get better balance. She felt a hand intrude itself between her legs and take hold of one of the little gold discs that dangled there.

The first man said something to the second man in Russian. Amanda thought that she heard the word 'Grobgy', which, of course, was the name on her discs, the name of her owner. Maybe they would return her to him.

The men talked some more. Her back began to ache from leaning forward so far without support. She was fighting off tears.

The hand returned to her loins and she felt it begin to massage her denuded love lips. Like all other slave girls, she had been trained to almost instant response. It did not take long for her crevasse to begin to moisten. She tried to suppress her moan of incipient lust, but she was not successful. She heard more laughter behind her.

"Okay," the second man said. "Straighten up." She did as she was told, ashamed that she would melt so quickly before these unknown men who clearly did not have her best interests at heart.

There was some more discussion between them. Some decision was reached. The first man went to the back of the trailer. "Lie down," the other one told her.

It was starting to get cold and the poor slave girl shivered. She saw a piece of trash go eddying up in the air as the night wind, a harbinger of the winter winds to come, tossed it carelessly about. Suppressing a sob, she brought herself down into a crouch and then fell backwards. When she was laying flat, her legs pressed defensively together, the first man came back. He was holding something in his hands.

Without ceremony, the second man, the driver, the younger one, grabbed her ankles and brought her legs up into the air. He then pulled them apart so that her labia were fully exposed and pushed them back until her rear end lifted a little from the ground. The other man crouched down between her legs and she felt a tugging on her right love lip and then a snap of metal. Then she felt the same thing on her left. She knew what the man was doing. He was removing her discs so that no one would know who she belonged to. Before he applied her new discs to her body, he leaned over her and showed one of them to her. His face was scarred and looked full of venom. She could just make out the design etched on the disc in the dim light as he dangled it over her face between her legs. There was a picture of a scorpion on it, its poisonous tail lifted as if to strike. Beneath that was the name, Zukerov.

"See that, my little whore," the man said ominously to her in English. "You belong to Zukerov now. I hope you like to fuck because you'll be doing a lot of it. If you don't give your best, the scorpion will sting you."

Amanda gave a little sob in reply. The man grinned, an ugly, vile looking grin, and then went back to his work. As she felt the new rings being run through the holes in the bottom of her labia, she began to cry all over again. When the man was done, she was pulled up to her feet and dragged to the end of the trailer. The door was open and a dim light shined overhead. There were ten small cages inside, in rows along both sides of the trailer, each with a gagged woman in it. All except one.

"You see," Zukerov said. "We just have room for you. We sold one yesterday. Maybe if you're lucky some rich man will fuck you and want to buy you. If you're not lucky, then, like I said, you'll do a lot of fucking. We have about sixty miles to travel tonight before we camp. When we stop for the night, after dinner, I'll give you ten lashes and then you can show me how good you fuck."

Amanda cringed at the thought of a whipping from this vile man. Nine forlorn pairs of eyes looked out at her. Each woman was gagged, as she was, and her hands were bound behind her back. Amanda rebelled at the thought of becoming one of them.

She tried to run, but the man took hold of the ring in her collar and yanked her back. "Ten more strokes for that, cunt," he told her.

Zukerov dragged her into the trailer and then to the empty cage on the right, all the way in the back. It was small. He unlocked the door with a special tool and swung it down. Then, he pushed her in. When her feet were fully inside, he brought up the door to the cage and locked it again. Amanda struggled to right herself in the cage. She was lying on her bound hands behind her and her legs were in the air. There was just room enough to turn herself around so that she was kneeling on the steel plate that was the cage's floor. There was a drain in the middle of it so she could pee if she had to. The cage was so small that when she finally attained her knees, she had to bend her neck.

"See you later, whore," Zukerov told her. He walked down the line of cages and turned out the light. The door to the trailer closed and Amanda and the other nine, unhappy women were sealed into utter darkness. As the trailer began to move, she started crying again.

CHAPTER SEVEN

Grobgy, for the first time in almost a week, awoke in his own bed. He had had a great time at the Fall Tournament, except for the last part, of course. He had spent his days watching the nubile ponies strut their stuff and, in between, sampling the plentitude of slave girls that dashed here and there around the festival grounds. He always brought fifteen or twenty of his own stock with him and he and the other estate owners swapped them back and forth like trading cards. He wasn't sure how many of the original sluts he had brought down with him he had come back with. The stewards would go through them today, seeing which ones were his and which ones were from other estates. They would change the tags on the new girls just as the tags would be changed on any of his whores who had gotten swept up by the other estate owners.

It was good to shuffle the girls like a deck of cards once in a while. You always hated giving up the best of the lot, but life would get very dull if you didn't have a steady diet of fresh flesh. Take the girl in bed with him now. Her name was Cheryl or Shirley or something like that. He would have to take a look at her chest later just to make sure he got it right. She was a shapely brunette, with long, chestnut colored hair that reached down to her waist. She was thin, but had heavy, full breasts and wide hips. She took well to the whip too, as the long red marks on her body that he had put there last night attested to. When he had finished fucking her last night, he had bound her wrists to her ankles and put a slave hood over her head. Her feet and hands were up in the air above her back. He knew she was awake because he saw her fingers nervously twitching as his movements revealed to her that he had arisen.

He always started the day with a good fuck. He pushed her sideways so that she was lying on her side, facing him. Her beautiful breasts just begged for abuse. He reached out and caught her nipples between his pointer fingers and his thumbs and gave them a fierce pinch. The girl moaned in pain. He kept it up, though, squeezing harder and harder and twisting them until the girl's moans became cries. "She's really awake now," he thought. Her agony had made him hard.

He knew that he should just tear off a piece and get on with his day; he had things to do. The number one thing was to settle Drabik's hash. He was pleased when the killer had reported the fulfillment of retribution against that ass of a ponygirl driver, but that certainly wasn't enough to divert Grobgy from his intents. Drabik had to go, but first, he would enjoy some of the fruits of his callous rule over his criminal empire.

It hadn't always been like this. As a KGB sergeant, he had started off by running whores for the benefit of his masters, the higher ups who never got their hands dirty. It was a small step to running whores on the streets. The KGB dungeons always had a ready supply of young girls who would rather spread their legs than get twenty years in a labor camp. And if there weren't enough in the basement cells of the Lubyanka, he could always pick a few up at the university which was usually teeming with counterrevolutionary activity.

Then came the downfall of the worker's state. He had enough cash put aside to buy into a few of the nascent capitalistic enterprises. His partners always found themselves shortly eased out or floating in the Moskya River. The colonels and generals believed that they could muscle in on his good fortune, too stupid to have feathered their beds appropriately. One by one, he had gotten rid of them or otherwise moved them off the stage. Like most organizations, the KGB was run by its noncoms and the men under him were as loyal as apostles.

Those were the good old days. He had a different whore every night. He had cornered the heroin trade and dozens of strung out models, actresses and party girls lay down on their backs for him to ensure a steady supply. Most of them he had whored out sooner or later. And he had an ironclad rule. Once a girl became one of his whores, she gave up the drug scene or he knew some fellows who took delight in finding out how much agony they could inflict on a female before she gave up the ghost.

He released the young girl's meaty breasts and she gave out an anguished sigh. Her face was covered by her hood. He tried to remember what she looked like. If he wasn't wrong, she had a long, thin face and an aquiline nose, a little too long for classic beauty, but not so much that her face wasn't pleasant to behold.

Grobgy leaned over and took one of the girl's tormented teats in his mouth. He spread her legs with his left hand and ran it across her taut belly. It was soft, silky soft, but firm. The girl shivered just a little bit as he suckled on her long, thin nipple. His hand dropped lower and he delved it between her outstretched thighs. The skin of her puss was as soft as a baby's cheek. She had taken good care of herself. He tickled the apex of her slit and then ran his fingers along its length, back and forth, until the well trained strumpet began to lubricate. He paused in his oral devotion to her breast to look at the two inch high, blue, Cyrillic writing over her chest. He had been right. Her name was Cheryl. A pretty name. American maybe? It didn't matter. He wondered whose property she had been before falling into his clutches. He slipped his hand from her moistening quim and took hold of one of the golden disks that dangled from her labia. There was an etching of a boar on it, with large tusks. It was Rajinsky's emblem. He ran a clearinghouse for stolen securities and had an interest, enforced at the end of a pistol, in several large banks back in the Russian Republic. He wondered which one of his beauties he had traded for her. Rajinsky was a notoriously hard bargainer and he was sure it was one of his best whores. Well, this one would have to prove herself sufficiently entertaining to warrant the exchange or she would rue the day she had ever met Axmail Grobgy. Who knew, maybe she did already.

The heavyset, black bearded gangster released the glittering disc and slid his fingers once more along the tender divide of the girl's sex. She gave out a little sigh of pleasure. "Good!" he thought. She was getting into the spirit of the thing.

He rolled the bound slave girl back to her belly and released her ankles from each other. When she rolled her to her side and then to her back, she was able to lie flat comfortably and to spread her legs more widely. He had left the connections between her wrist bracelets and her ankles in place and so her hands were denied her and her legs were pulled up, her knees high. He pushed her knees wider apart and inserted himself between them. There was nothing like the taste of pussy before breakfast, he thought.

He leaned his bearded face forwards and licked his fat tongue the length of the girl's dilated slash. Her hips writhed and she gave another deep sigh. Burying his face against her crevasse, he absorbed her tender nether lips into his mouth and suckled on them. The taste and aroma of her exciting loins enflamed him. He ran his tongue to the steeple of her delicious cathedral and toyed with the little bell ringer there until the girl gave a deep moan. He looked up. Her chest had broken out in a sweat and her nipples were taut and hard. Her breathing had become heavy. He leaned back down and took her clit between his teeth and bit down on it. Not so hard that there was any danger of ripping it off, but hard enough to turn the slut's moans of pleasure into ones of pain. Her back arched and her knees shook.

"Ooooooooooouuuummmm! Oooooouuuuuuuuummm!" she moaned. Her knees pressed against his shoulders in a vain attempt to deny him access to her coosh. He released the stiff nubbin and gave it a few hot licks with his tongue until the girl's hips began their lust inspired motions again and then he bit it once more, harder this time. The girl's moans were even louder and, for a moment, he thought he felt her body begin the forbidden effort of seeking to deny him his pleasure in her pain by escaping his clutches. If she forgot her training enough to do that, she would truly be sorry.

The bear like man released her clit once more, giving her respite. His cock was hard and needy now. He rose on the large, soft, luxurious bed and placed his hips between her thighs. He aimed his thick cock at her gate and pushed it forwards. It shoved aside her engorged love lips easily and slid inside her. The heat of her slippery tunnel made him sigh with pleasure. She was tight and he felt her moving her inner muscles to please him. She was well trained indeed.

Once he began a steady, forceful series of thrusts in and out of her flush canal, she began to rock her hips to meet his downward strokes. Her hooded head swayed back and forth in her excitement. Grobgy stared down at her featureless face. "I wonder where she's gone," he thought. "Some place where warmth and love and caring exist, no doubt, enough for her to stoke her fires. Perhaps some distant lover, or some imaginary one." Slave girls needed a place to go when in the hands of even the most brutal master, for if they were found nonresponsive, their lives could get unhappy very quickly.

Grobgy was nearing his crisis. The girl was making little mewing sounds, signaling the nearness of her explosion of lust. He wanted to make it last. He slowed himself gradually until his cock came to a practical halt, the tip of his rigid cock lying just outside the door to her womb. The girl's body squirmed and her feet pressed down hard on the mattress. Her breasts swayed and trembled as her deep breaths of passion animated them. Her whole body tensed.

Slowly, but surely, Grobgy sunk himself back down inside her. Her pussy welcomed him, its moist heat delighting his member and sending a wave of pleasure through him. His pace quickened. Shortly, he resumed his solid, powerful thrusts. The girl was crying out from behind her gag. He felt her body convulse and her pussy's walls grab at his meat. It was all he needed.

"Arrrrrrgh! Arrrrrrrgh!" he bellowed into the vast room, his deep, gravelly voice echoing off of the well appointed walls. "Arrrrrrrgh! Arrrrrgh!" he shouted.

The girl's body squirmed and contorted as her passions flowed. It was like riding a snake, her torso shifting this way and that. The contractions of her quim went on and on, bringing him echoes of his pleasure long after his prick had finished dousing her womb with its thick, creamy, white sauce.

"Ahhhhhh!" Grobgy exclaimed as he let himself collapse on the whore's body. On most days, he filled his whores' cavities five or six times a day. This was just his start. Often he selected one of them to be his 'special companion' bearing the brunt of his passion for abuse while he released his lusts in the bodies of others. He had already decided that he would keep this one with him for a few days. She had depths he had not explored yet. So far, she had been gagged when he abused her. Later, this afternoon, he would whip her with her mouth free, whip her with the thin, fierce whip that made a whore's skin tatter. She would scream, perhaps even beg for surcease. He would look forward to it.

But now, he had business to attend to. It was already almost 10:30. He chided himself. In the old days, he was up at the break of dawn, ready to take the actions necessary to feed his growing empire. Nowadays, he was less fierce in his pursuit of fortune. He had many millions and had lost the fierce hunger for more. Life was good,

Grobgy rose from the bed, leaving the panting slave girl in place. He would have one of the stewards come by later and free her so that she could relieve her needs, eat and clean her body for him. He would leave word that she should remain hooded and gagged except when she needed to use her mouth. He wanted her nice and ripe with fear and unhappiness when he whipped her.

He threw on his large, soft, dark red, cotton robe. It had a fur collar and went down to his ankles. When he dressed in it, he felt regal. Slipping on his leather sandals, he strode from his bedroom and down the central stairway. One of the slave girls was waiting there for him with a pot of fresh coffee on a tray and several sweet roles. He opened the door to his office and she followed him in.

He thought that he recognized her. She was named Renka and had blond hair. Polish, he thought, or maybe German. She was a little more broad of shoulder than was optimal in a slave girl, but her breasts were nice and round and she had pouting lips. He would have to remember her.

Grobgy sat behind his huge, oaken desk while the slave girl poured out his coffee into a large mug. He used to take it black, but now he liked a little cream and sugar in it. The slave girl dutifully doctored the coffee to his liking and then, putting aside her tray, knelt down on the floor next to his desk to await his pleasures.

Grobgy picked up the handset to his shiny, gold and ivory telephone. "Get me Vronsky," he snarled. Vronsky was his security chief. He had already spoken about his plans for Drabik with him. He wanted to give him the go ahead.

The male servant on the telephone answered, "Mr. Vronsky is on his way up to your office, sir,"

"Okay then," Grobgy growled and hung up the phone.

He was starting on his second sweet roll when the door to his office opened. He looked up and saw Vronsky, a well dressed, slim, weasel looking man. Just the man to put a bullet behind Drabik's ear.

"Vronsky…" Grobgy started. His voice trailed off. Following Vronsky into the room was none other than Drabik himself. Both of the men were armed and two other of his security guards followed them. Grobgy knew immediately that he was about to die. He put the sweet roll back down on the plate.

"So, it's time," he said to none of them in particular. Looking at Drabik, he said, "I guess I waited too long. I should have had you shot six months ago."

"Yes, Axmail, you should have," Drabik returned. "Are you going to give us trouble? If so, I'll shoot you right here in the gut. It'll take a long time to die. Cooperate and it'll all be over in a few minutes, nice and clean."

There was a pistol in Grobgy's desk drawer, but he knew that he would never have time to get it out. He believed Drabik when he said he could make it long and hard or quick and easy. "Why not die with dignity?" he thought. "I've had my day."

"I'd like to get dressed first," Grobgy said.

"No." was all Drabik replied.

Grobgy resigned himself to dying looking like a character from a French bedroom farce.

"Let's do it then," he said.

The slave girl was looking up at the men and their guns. She was shivering with fear. Drabik looked at her. "She's mine now," he thought.

"Stay here," he told her. "Put your head to the floor and your hands behind you. I'll be back later to give you a good fuck. If you've moved an inch, I'll skin you alive."

The girl whined and put her forehead on the soft, luxurious rug. She crossed her hands behind her as instructed. She cursed herself for being in the wrong place at the wrong time.

"Come on," Drabik ordered. "Let's get this over with."

Grobgy rose to his full 6'4" height. He knew that he could break Drabik in half, but that he would never get the chance. Then a thought occurred to him. "Anya..." he started.

"Don't worry," Drabik snapped back. "I'll be taking care of her."

Grobgy sighed. He had protected her all these years and now this. At least, he hoped, it would be quick for her too. Somehow, though, given what he knew about Drabik, he doubted it. Well, there was nothing he could do.

He stepped from behind the desk and pulled the robe tighter around his body. The men all stepped back to let him pass, keeping just far enough away from him so that he would not have the opportunity to grab one of their weapons. When he stepped into the hall, he saw four more of Vronsky's men waiting. Drabik had all his ducks in a line. He had to give him that.

Like a little parade, the men marched down the wide, circular stairway to the ground floor. Drabik motioned him to go out the back way and he complied.

There was a copse of woods about a hundred yards from the mansion. He was directed there. Two other men were waiting and there was a van parked nearby, presumably to take his mortal remains to a more appropriate resting place somewhere out on the steppes. He was about to kneel on the ground when Drabik spoke to him.

"Take off the robe," he spit out.

Grobgy looked at him. Well, he came into the world naked, why not go out that way? Drabik was right. There was no sense getting his blood all over it.

He drew the garment off his shoulders and threw it aside. He knelt on the soft grass. Drabik stepped behind him quickly. All Grobgy heard was the click of the hammer being pulled back and then everything went black.

* * * * * * * * * * * * * * *

A half hour later, after spreading word via telephone to other members of his conspiracy to make their moves, Drabik headed down to the ponybarn. When he entered it, there was a tall, svelte, black haired beauty in the middle of the room standing on the tippy toes of her shiny, black boots, her hands tied and held up over her head,.

"Hello, Anya," he said.

Anya had been distracted by a fierce looking whip that one of the men in the barn held. Her mouth was covered with tape, so she had nothing to say, nothing intelligible anyway, when she saw him.

The black haired beauty did go into a little dance and make loud murmuring sounds from behind her taped lips. Her eyes were as angry as a rabid hound's.

"I see that you're glad to see me, Anya. Well, I'm glad to see you too. I told you we would get together after the tournament, but I'm guessing that this isn't what you had in mind."

This drove Anya into another spate of angry words, all muffled by her gag. Drabik had stepped near her and she swung one of her booted feet out at him, nearly hitting his leg. He deftly stepped aside. The men in the barn laughed.

"That's not very nice, Anya," Drabik told her. She was dressed in her trademark white, silk blouse and a pair of tight, black slacks. Her long, straight, black hair was down over her shoulders. She had pale skin, almost white. But her face, at this moment, was red with the force of her anger.

"If you promise not to kick me, I'll take the tape off of your lips, Anya. How about that? You can tell me what's on your mind."

Anya calmed just a little and nodded at the killer. As soon as Drabik tore the tape off, she emitted a torrent of words.

"You bastard! You have no right to do this to me! My father will have you burning on a spit in an hour, all of you!" She cast her angry glance around the open area of the barn. "Let me down this instant! Untie me and let me down!" Her toes did a little two step as she tried to stay anchored to the floor. Her chest heaved with her rage making her plentiful breasts sway and jerk amusingly behind her tight, snow white blouse.

"I'm afraid I'm not going to do that, Anya, at least not yet," Drabik answered as he stepped back from her. "And I'm afraid that you father isn't going to come and help you. Right now his corpse is on its way to its final resting place. So, you see, you had better learn better manners or you are surely going to suffer."

Anya was shocked by the news, but she didn't spend any time mourning for her 'Papa'. She went right to work on Drabik.

"Oh, Anton," she said, "we can finally be together! No more skulking around like two adolescents! I've been waiting for this day for the longest time!"

"No, I'm afraid that we're not going to be together, Anya. It's true that things are going to change for you, but I don't think you're going to very happy about it."

"W,what do you mean, Anton? I love you! Don't you know that?"

"You love only yourself Anya," Drabik retorted. "You have a black heart, perhaps as black as mine. Unfortunately, I'm the one with the power now and I will be making all of the decisions."

"Oh, yes, Anton, yes!" Anya shouted desperately. "I understand that! I'll do whatever you want! I'm yours!"

Drabik laughed. He looked around at the other men, rough looking ponygirl trainers and their assistants. They were all smiling broadly.

"You heard what she said, didn't you?" Drabik asked them. "She's mine. What greater declaration of slavery could she make?"

"S,slavery?" Anya asked fearfully. "You're not serious Anton, are you? After all that we've meant to each other? P,please Anton, don't do anything like that!" A definite whine had entered her voice. Her eyes were widened and her breathing had become heavy. Her hands twisted in their bindings above her. She knew that Drabik always meant what he said. He wasn't prone to practical jokes.

"Well, not actually slavery, Anya. We've had such fun romping in our little hideaway for the last nine months or so. You so loved dressing up as a ponygirl that I thought that I would make you into a ponygirl for real."

"Ohhhhhhhhhhh!" Anya cried out in despair. She danced on her toes and tried to yank at the bindings to her wrists. "Pleeeeeeease, Anton! Pleeeeeeease! Don't do that! I'll be your slave girl! You can do anything you want to me! But please don't turn me into a ponygirl, pleeeease!"

Drabik stepped up to the frantic woman and took a tight hold of a sheath of her hair at the back of her head. Anya moaned from the pain. Tears had started to form in her eyes and her lips were quivering.

"Frightened, Anya?" Drabik asked her, his voice cold and hard. "You should be. You see, even if I made you into a slave girl, I could never trust you. My men told me that you ordered them to bury that poor little slave girl, Natalie, alive. Now they usually do what they're told. But why waste a good slave girl? They figured they would have a little fun with her first. Then she told them how you had been plotting to get at Lightning. They brought her to me right away. She told me all about your orders to her to get close to Jerzi's slave girl and promise her anything if she would hurt her. Too bad for you she did so prematurely."

"Oh, Anton, I'm sorry! I'm sorry!" Anya shouted desperately. "I was jealous! I admit it! It's just that I love you so! I wanted you to be with me!"

"There you go with that love thing again, Anya. I'm afraid love is not a word that's in your vocabulary. Now, I could have forgiven you your little failed escapade with Natalie, although having her buried alive was very nasty thing to do, but, you see, I know what you did with Gregor. Before he died, he talked. Since he's dead, he can't testify at any inquiry, but its good enough for me to pronounce sentence on you!"

"No, Anton! No!" Anya screamed. "I did it for us! For you! You were obsessed by the pony! She cast a spell on you! I freed you from it! Please don't do this, please!"

Drabik's ire rose to a new pitch. He knew that there was only one way to end his obsession with the champion ponygirl: with his hands around her neck, squeezing the life out of her. He released the tall, young woman's hair and stepped back. "Good bye, Anya," he said. "In a few moments Anya Grobgy will have disappeared. All that will be left is a black haired pony with no name. Should I give you your old name back once you've been dehumanized, Anya? I think maybe I will."

Drabik nodded to the men who were sitting around the terrorized, young woman. They jumped up and immediately went to work.

One man drew a belt around the unhappy woman's thighs while another jammed a gag into her mouth, a round, black ball with a tube leading to a little bulb. It was some job getting it in. Anya screamed and struggled, trying to fling her head this way and that to avoid the heinous instrument. But when the first man had finished fastening her graceful thighs together, he and a third man leant some assistance. Her head was held captive by one while the other used both his hands to force her jaw open. It didn't need to open far, for at this stage, the black ball was rather small. Once it had popped in, the second man gave the bulb at the end of the tube several hard squeezes. The ball in her mouth inflated immediately. Her eyes widened in surprise and terror and she ceased, momentarily, her struggles. Once the ball was fully inflated, way past the point where she could possibly hope to shove it out of her mouth with her tongue, the tube was removed and the little air hole in the gag was turned closed.

"Mmmmmmmmmmm! Mmmmmmmmmmmm!" Anya screamed looking at Drabik desperately. She had said her last words as a human being.

It didn't take long to denude her. Once her boots were off, the tight slacks came down. She wore no panties and her trim, black bush was exposed, to the merriment of her assailants. Anya had treated most of them with scorn and disdain on many occasions. They were anxious to give her her comeuppance.

The belt around Anya's thighs had to be temporarily removed, but once her black slacks were tugged down past her knees, it was reinstalled. When the pants were slipped off of her feet, another belt went around her ankles.

Her blouse was even easier. Using a sharp knife, one of the men merely shredded it until it could be ripped from her body in pieces. She was wearing a dainty bra, sufficient to hold her well developed mammaries in place. Off it came in a jiffy and her orbs swung free to everyone's delight.

Drabik, of course, had seen her tits often, but the other men had been deprived of that pleasure until now. It had not been uncommon for one or more of them to stare as she rode by on her fine charger, her heavy globes recording each step of the horse. There had been much speculation as to their size and heft, not to mention the hue and size of her areola. Now everyone knew for sure.

The first accouterment of her new life that was affixed to her body was the sturdy ponygirl collar. While one of the men had hold of her hair to keep her still, another presented it to her pretty, pale throat. It made an ominous sound of finality when it clicked closed. It would not be removed again except for the occasional washing of her neck.

The next to go on were her pony boots. Anya was squirming and twisting frantically in a vain attempt to avoid her fate. It was difficult to hold her legs still long enough so that one of the men could slide them on her feet, but these men were experts at what they did and that problem was soon overcome by two hardfisted blows to her thighs, making her moan with pain. After that, the naked woman hung limply from her bound hands and it was easy to lift first one foot and then the other to apply them. Once strapped to her calves, the boots were hooked together, rendering her feet immobile once more.

Since the ponygirl collar had a strap going down the back to which her wrists would be affixed, it was time to lower her hands from up above her. Once there was enough slack in the rope holding her wrists aloft, one of the men kicked her feet out from underneath her and she fell to knees. Another man pushed her pale, enticing torso to the ground, breasts down, and mounted her, his knee pressed into the small of her back.

Once her hands were free, they were drawn behind her, one by one, and locked into the strap that ran down her back. Her hands were now, and would hence forever be, useless instruments.

This seemed to respark Anya's desperate fervor. She squirmed and contorted her body, shouting from behind her gag, sounds that emerged as muffled syllables. This was the source of great amusement, for the time to struggle had long ago ended. The men even stepped back to allow her to explore the limitations of her bindings for herself. Her black hair was all askew and sweat had broken out on her chest. Her breasts had picked up some of the dust from the floor which was smearing as her perspiration ran down over them.

There is some debate as to when a woman actually loses her personhood when she is converted to a ponygirl. Some assert that it's when she is first collared. Others insist that it's when her hands are locked forever behind her. But for most, it was when her head was shaved and she was first adorned with her pony hood. Since that was still a stage away, Drabik felt free to issue some words of torment to the dismally unhappy, young woman.

"I must say that I expected more of a struggle from you Anya. I'm disappointed. Maybe you secretly wanted to be a ponygirl all along. You used to get all hot and bothered when I used to dress you up. Sometimes I thought that you would never stop coming. Think how lucky you'll be now. I'd guess that you're going to get a lot of cocks over the next few days. I've told the boys how skittish you were about ass fucking. They've promised me that they will get you over that right away."

Anya was looking up at her former lover. Her face was a mask of fear and anguish. "Mmmmmmmmm!" she called out her desperate plea to the dark killer. Her moan was plaintive, as piteous as ever had been uttered by a human female undergoing conversion. Tears were streaming down her face. For a moment, Drabik felt a pang of sympathy for her. After all, she was going from the queen of the walk to a lowly beast. It would be hard for anyone.

One of the men had brought out the electric shears that would be used to doff Anya's beautiful, silky, black hair. Another was preparing a bowl of hot water so that her skull could be shaven clean. Anya looked up at them and moaned again. In her panic, she tried to rise and run away, but her struggle was unavailing as one of the men simply gave her a little shove with his boot and she was lying on the floor once more.

As if choreographed, the men sprang back into action. One of the men took hold of her hair at the back of her head and pulled her to her knees. She gave a mighty shriek of pain from behind her gag. Once she was kneeling up, the man circled her neck with his arm and held her firmly in place while another took hold of her long hair and pulled it from her head so that it could be shorn.

Anya struggled futilely as the third man began to shear off her locks. The black strands fell to the wooden barn floor in chunks. Soon, the second man was holding only that portion of her head's adornment that would remain, a long, shiny, black ponytail. Anya was crying now. Her hands squirmed in their confinements behind her back and her naked breasts fluttered as her body was wracked with sobs. Her head was tilted downwards so that the excess hair at the back could be shorn. Drabik saw two tears drip from her flooded eyes and drop down to the dusty floor. It meant nothing to him.

Now that her long locks had been reduced to stubble on her head, the fourth man brought forth the razor and the bowl of steamy, soapy water. He drew the razor along her pate and denuded it of all of the remaining growth but for her decorative ponytail. Anya had stopped struggling, knowing that it was useless. All the cruelties that she had inflicted on her father's slave girls and ponies over the years were rising in her mind. Would she be treated as cruelly and as callously as she had treated the others? There was no doubt of it.

When her head was smooth and shiny, she was released. Her once proud locks had been reduced to the skein of hair that descended from a small circle on the pate of her skull and down her back. She raised her head unhappily. She gave out another deep whine of despair when she saw one of the men hand Drabik a blue, neoprene ponyhood. It was, of course, for her.

Drabik took the hood in his hands and crouched down before the kneeling woman. He took her chin in his hand and took a long look at her.

"I just want to remember what you look like, Anya," he told her. "In a minute, your face will be sealed away forever. It's a pity that your temperament never matched its grace and beauty. Goodbye, Anya."

The terrified woman gave out a howl through her gag as Drabik stretched the fabric of the hood in his hands. He took hold of the ponytail that jutted behind her head and threaded it through the hole in the top of the hood. Then, without ceremony, he pulled the hood down over her face. He lined the little eyelets in the hood's base up with the small hooks in her collar and locked them in place. He leaned back and made a small adjustment so that the pony's nostrils were aligned properly with the gap meant for that purpose and so the little holes through which she would view the world from now on were settled properly over her eyes.

He rose and stepped back while two of the men took hold of her arms and brought her to her feet. Her solid boots thudded on the floor as she tried for balance. Her fear weakened knees made her legs sag. There were two more things to do before her conversion to a beast was fully complete.

The new ponygirl was dragged over to some bales of hay that lay against the wall. Her back was pressed down on it and, while the first two men held her shoulders down, two others lifted her knees and spread them, revealing the delicate slit between her thighs. Anya had always kept her bush neatly trimmed, so it was a quick, simple matter for the man with the bowl of soapy water and razor to swipe the remaining strips of stiff, black hair away. He ran his hand over her denuded pudenda, making sure that it was completely hairless and smooth. For the rest of her days as a ponygirl, she would undergo this ritual. He slipped his thumb up along her bare slit and tickled the nubbin of pleasure at its top. The new pony began to struggle again, knowing full well that her first rape as a dehumanized animal was about to commence.

Once her crevasse had given in to its involuntary excitement, the man was able to slip his thumb readily into the now moistened divide. When satisfied that the going was good, he stepped back and, looking back at the new master of the estate, smiled lewdly. It was the master's duty to break in all the new ponygirls. Drabik already had his thick wand extruding from his pants and was stroking it, making it nice and hard.

Without delay, Drabik advanced on the helpless pony. It looked up at him through its small windows on the world and moaned. He positioned himself between her wide-spread thighs and pressed the head of his cock against the enflamed lips of her sex. As he ran his piece up and down the sweet divide, he reveled in his revenge. No one fucked with Anton Drabik! No one! Not even the spoiled, venal daughter of a rich, powerful gangster.

The pony's thighs were shuddering from a combination of arousal and fear as he began to inch his prick inside her. He pressed forwards slowly, making sure that the pony felt her personhood slipping away, centimeter by centimeter. When his cock was buried to its hilt, his hands pressed down on either side of her hooded head, and he began the motions that would produce the pony's first orgasm as a beast.

While her slit had been well used, it was still tight. He felt the pleasure of the coitus spread through his body. All of his machinations of the last few months were coming to fruition. All the tension of waiting, plotting, fearfully hoping that his plot would not be revealed to the former KGB sergeant was being released. Each thrust of his thick rod brought him incremental satisfaction until he was soon pounding his hips against the crux of the pony's thighs.

The former Anya was squirming and moaning as the cock of her owner assailed her. She had shut her eyes, trying to blot out the vision of her disgrace and abasement.

She tried to fight off the gnawing rise of her arousal, dismal at the thought of the amusement she was bringing to her father's former servants. Her efforts were futile. The rasping of the rigid manhood along the walls of her steamy tunnel made her lusts grow higher and higher. The hands that held her down, that held her thighs spread wide, burned into her. Soon, all that her mind could focus on was her developing passion and the need for its completion. "Ohhhh! Ohhhhh!" she moaned behind her gag. Her legs and hips had taken on a life of their own, shaking and squirming as her heat came near to boil.

Drabik sensed the readiness of his new thrall to her crisis. He sawed his thick member back and forth frantically, bringing his own lusts closer and closer to termination. When the pony began to shake and moan and he felt her cunt throb around his prick, he allowed himself release. Issuing a triumphant groan, he poured his spunk into the pony's belly. Wave after wave of pleasure coursed through him. At last! At last! He was victorious! Ruler of a thousand men, lord over a vast criminal empire, master of a thousand whores in and out of Kalikastan, he roared his exaltation. It echoed inside the vast ponybarn. All the ponies in their stalls, awaiting the pleasure of the men who controlled them, cringed nervously at the sound. A new era had begun.

* * * * * * * * * * * * * *

Drabik spent the rest of the day at Grobgy's old desk coordinating the developments all around his new empire. Most of Grobgy's enterprises had fallen without any trouble and fifteen of the twenty or so men who Drabik knew would never accept him as their leader had been rounded up and shot. The others were in hiding with huge bounties on their heads. Sooner or later, they would join their friends in gangster heaven.

The slave girl who had been in Grobgy's office earlier that morning had spent the day serving him, benefiting from a good round fuck or two when things were going well and suffering the brunt of her new master's displeasure when they were not. The new ponygirl received, under Drabik's supervision, her first whipping, one that she would remember as long as she lived, and was then taken out by one of the trainers to the training ring to begin her first workout. She would be named and tattooed tomorrow. Drabik had reconsidered giving her back her old name. She was a pony now and it would be unfair to have her bear an appellation that would remind him of her evil deeds back when she was a woman. She should be judged from here on solely on her performance as a beast. He had decided on the name 'Happy'.

All day long, the thought of Lightning being in the possession of the Americans burned him. There was nothing he could do about it for the time being. Tomorrow, after he had made sure that everything was in order and he had issued his commands for the day, he would make the thirteen hour drive to the Burnham estate. Once there, Burnham would either give him the ponygirl or suffer the consequences.

CHAPTER EIGHT

Michael Burnham stared out the window of his luxurious office on the second floor of his mansion. He was watching with some impatience the carriage house on the other side of the large expanse of grass that served as a kind of courtyard for the estate. The carriage house was, and had been since they arrived in Kalikastan, the headquarters of Jake's crew. They were in there now and he was waiting for them to make the first move.

It would have been a simple thing to have Borodin's men storm the small dwelling, small, that is, by the standards of the mansion. But for some reason he had decided to let Jake act first. He and Jake went back a long way. He had done some very difficult jobs for him, producing almost miraculous results and, when you came down to it, Burnham owed him a lot. It just seemed to satisfy his own perverted sense of justice to wait. Once Jake made a move to rescue the ponygirls, he would, technically, be crossing the line into unauthorized activity. Burnham was still, nominally, his boss and Lightning and Chocolate were his property. It was Jake's duty to reveal his plan for the rescue to Burnham and to obtain approval. By acting without authority, Jake would be making himself an outlaw.

Waiting was not Burnham's forte. He was a man of action and always grabbed what he wanted when he wanted it. He was actually proud of himself for his restraint. In his own mind, it was a mark of character and a measure of the heights to which his enterprises in Kalikastan had brought him. He saw himself as some latter day feudal lord vying for empire.

Behind him, kneeling near his broad, ornately carved oaken desk, was his birdwoman, Betty. He had removed her locked gag from her mouth since there was no way that she could warn Jake now. He had needed to use her oral cavity to relieve some of the tension a little while ago and saw no reason to restore the silencing instrument.

The ponybarn that housed the subjects of this Mexican standoff was about a hundred yards from Burnham's window and an equal distance from the carriage house. The two star ponygirls were locked down, flat on their backs, so that their wounds could heal. He had not yet availed himself of their flesh as was his right as their owner. He wanted to wait until Jake and his men had been disposed of so that his celebration would be complete. He had barred his men from making use of the ponies until he had had first licks.

Some part of him still maintained a moral qualm about fucking his own niece. Maybe that's why he wanted Jake out of the way first, he thought. Other than Borodin, his security chief, and Betty, but she was of no moment, only Jake and his men knew of his relationship to the champion pony. No one else in Kalikastan would find fault with him for fucking his own property.

As to the minor qualm, it had been reducing in size ever since the thought that it had occurred to him he would be crazy to lose the opportunity to own the two fastest ponygirls in Kalikastan. His mind was filled lately with visions of Lightning's beautiful, pale body, her bountiful, exquisite breasts, the delicate folds of her denuded sex. He wanted to possess her totally, regardless of any and all taboos. And he would do it too, but first he had to get Jake and his boys out of the way.

* * * * * * * * * * * * * *

As Burnham was peering out of his window at the carriage house, Jake was inside peering out at the mansion. It was almost time to make his move. The sun was dipping in the west and it would be dark in about an hour. Martinez was scheduled to pick them up at a landing zone about a mile from the estate just after dusk. Flying out of the country in the growing darkness would make it more difficult for any air pursuit to find them. Jake figured that it would take about ten minutes to secure the two ponies and then another ten minutes to run the mile to the LZ. That meant that the fireworks should begin in about ten minutes.

He and Irving had spent the day before hiding out at the farmhouse where the tranquillizer rifles had been stored. About an hour ago, they had loaded them into the trunk of their car and entered the estate by the rear entrance in the hopes of throwing off Borodin's security men. He had thought that they might have to zip the guards who were normally stationed there, but, to his surprise, the entrance was unguarded. They had driven up to the carriage house where Tucker, Curley and Leon were waiting.

From his perch in the second story of the carriage house, looking out the window of what had been his bedroom for the last seven months or so, he could see three of Borodin's men guarding the outside of the barn. The dinner gong had sounded about ten minutes ago and all the trainers and the security men who were not on guard duty had headed to the bunkhouse for their meal. Curly and Leon were charged with setting of a gas bomb in the barracks that would incapacitate anyone inside. Tucker would get the three ponygirls, Lightning, Chocolate and Czarina, the former and soon again to be Maddy, Jackie and Maureen, out of their stalls and ready to make the dash to the LZ. Irving and Jake would stand watch, making sure no one interfered with their operation using the M-16's they would recover from the incapacitated guards. A million things could go wrong, but it was their best shot.

Jake's pretty, black haired slave girl, Dana, was squatting in her cage at the foot of his bed. She was bound and gagged, but her eyes told him that she knew that something was up. He had had her give oral comfort to his cock about a half hour ago, just to take the edge off of his tension, and then locked her back in her cage. Part of him wished that he could take her with him. He knew he could not. Success depended on there being no huge storm of publicity after the ponies' liberation. It was the only way that he could hope that the Kalikastani gangsters wouldn't hunt them all down in revenge. They would risk public exposure of the horrors of their little land and all hell would break lose. The conspiracy of silence between them and the American and other Western governments would be broken. The National Commission would have nothing left to lose if word of the rescue of kidnapped and enslaved American women hit the news. Jake was certain that he could finesse the return of Maddy and Maureen to the world. Maureen was likely to remain silent for Irving's sake. Maddy would do the same for her own and Jackie, well, no one had missed Jackie when she was taken and no one would be surprised when she came back. She had no intention of returning to her Chicago haunts anyway.

But if Dana or any other of the slave girls were freed, there would no guarantee that they wouldn't tell the New York Times or CNN all about what had happened to them. With each freed person, the risk of exposure was heightened geometrically. No, Dana had to stay. It was too bad, but her fate would be no worse, or better, than the five thousand or so innocent young women who were held in bondage in the country. Jake hadn't come to Kalikastan to save them anyway.

The one thing that bothered Jake was that he could not get in touch with Mary Ellen, the beautiful, statuesque lesbian who, together with her band of fellow lefties, he had left in charge of the Jersey slaving operation. It had been agreed in advance that the operation would be shut down and wound up by now, but he could not get any confirmation. Irving had jury rigged a cell phone so that they could make calls out of the country and there was no answer on Mary Ellen's line. He hoped that there hadn't been a fuck up.

The sun dipped below the roof of the ponybarn some hundred yards away and Jake looked at his watch. It was time to go.

Like clockwork, Curly and Leon came into his bedroom armed with the tranquillizer rifles and carrying one for him. The best angle at the guards outside the ponybarn was from Jake's windows. It was important that all three guards go down at the same time. Next to Jake and Martinez, who was busy elsewhere, Curley and Leon were the best shots. Irving waited downstairs, his eyes glued to the bunkhouse through a pair of binoculars, just to make sure that none of the other security men came out to spoil their fun. Tucker was with him.

Jake nudged the window open. Curley and Leon did the same to the one next to him. Jake gave them a nod and took aim with the powerful rifle. He had practiced yesterday while at the farmhouse and Leon and Curley had taken some practice shots out the back windows of the carriage house a little while ago. The results had been mixed, but that was the way it went. There was no more time to practice.

Jake had assigned the guards in the middle and to the left to Curley and Leon. He was to take the one on the right. He took a deep breath, bringing the black clad man within the cross hairs. "Now!" he whispered urgently.

Three loud 'pop's sounded in the small room. Jake's man grabbed at his chest and went down. Jake looked up and saw Curley's man down too. Leon's man was looking at the others, apparently perplexed at what made them fall. Leon had missed! Jake saw the man look back at the carriage house and then start to run. Jake, Curley and Leon all got off their second shots within an instant. Two of the darts caught the man right in the back and he hit the ground.

The three men were off in a flash. They hustled down the stairs and out the front door. Irving gave them a sign that all was clear as they rushed by him.

Sprinting at maximum speed, the three men crossed the grassy quadrangle to the ponybarn in about 10 seconds. Irving and Tucker were close behind them. Leon and Curly, after sneaking their heads around the corner to make sure that on one would see them, made a dash for the bunkhouse where the gas bomb was all set up. Jake watched them go and then he and Tucker swung the huge ponybarn door open.

* * * * * * * * * * * * * *

Burnham had watched the Americans dash across the distance between the carriage house and the ponybarn. It was just as he thought. He picked up a wireless intercom device from his desk and pushed the button twice, the signal that Jake's men were on the move.

* * * * * * * * * * * * * *

When the barn door swung open, Jake saw that they were fucked. Standing there waiting for them was Burnham's security chief, Nicholai Borodin, and six of his men, all with their M-16's at the ready. Borodin had a wide grin on his face.

"Hello, Jake," he said, sardonically. "I guess the game is up, eh?"

The game was up. Burnham had outfoxed him again.

"Drop your weapons and put your hands on your heads," Borodin commanded.

The three men complied unhappily. One of Borodin's men came around behind them and tied off their hands behind their backs with coarse rope. Just then, Curley and Leon were led around the corner, their hands tied off too, sheepish looks upon their faces.

"It looks like it's a clean sweep," Borodin said tauntingly to Jake. "You Americans are so stupid with your cowboys and Indian games. I could have taken all five of you down as you crossed the quad, but Mr. Burnham said to take you alive. It seems he wants to say goodbye to you."

"Just get it over with," Jake shot out calmly. He had taken his chances and lost. He knew what happened to losers in his business. It was too bad that he would never see Tanya again, he thought.

"Come on," the tall, broad shouldered Russian snapped. "And you too," he directed at Irving. "Maybe Burnham will let you beg for your pitiful life." He laughed.

While Tucker, Curley and Leon were rounded up into the barn, Jake and Irving were marched off to the mansion. Apparently, the other men, the trainers and the rest of the security guards, had been told to stay in the barracks so that there wouldn't be too many witnesses. Not that it mattered. No one in Kalikastan would give too shits about what happened to Jake except Tanya and her family, but it was just good practice to keep those in the know to a minimum.

Jake trudged up the mansion stairway, his heart heavy. He had failed Maddy, failed Jackie, failed Maureen and Irving too. All those girls who had been transported to Kalikastan through the Jersey operation had suffered for nothing. He felt about as miserable as a man could feel. And now he was going to have to suffer the abuse of Burnham, the man who had become truly corrupted by Kalikastan and all the carnal delights that it offered.

The usually teeming mansion was empty except for the prisoners and their three guards. Burnham had put the entire place on lockdown pending the disposition of his 'problem'. Where normally slave girls would be scurrying around back and forth from their duty stations, corporate employees hustling to and fro with the latest financial data and corporate business, there were only empty chains connected to the poles and stanchions around the vast entrance hall.

When they reached Burnham's office, Borodin rang the buzzer that announced their arrival. Burnham buzzed them in.

"Hello, Jake," Burnham boomed expansively. "You've been a bad boy."

Jake was led to the center of the room in front of Burnham's desk. Burnham sat in front of him, a large glass of scotch in one hand, a chain leading to the ring in the front of Betty's collar in the other.

"You're the bad boy, Burnham, and you know it," Jake replied.

"Don't give me that shit, Jake," Burnham replied. "You know as well as I do that you're hip deep in this place too. Whose idea was it to take over the slaving operation in the States anyway? And how many slave girls have you fucked since you were here? How's that black haired bitch you keep up in your room? I'm going to enjoy busting her out before I send her to the barracks so the boys can have some fun with her."

Jake bristled at the realization that Dana would suffer because of him. It was another thing to chalk up to his failure.

"Oh, and one more thing, Jake," Burnham continued. "You're dike friend who was running the Jersey operation ran into a little problem. It seems that she and her girls found themselves housed in those same silver containers that they sent so many poor little girls to Kalikastan in. They'll all be here tomorrow. I'm going to make a six pony team out of them."

"So that's what happened to them," Jake thought. Well, they took their risks. It was just the way the ball bounced.

Borodin had taken a position to Jake's left. The other two security men had taken a position to Jake's back and to his extreme right. Irving was standing next to him.

"And you, Irving," Burnham continued, "you've destroyed my faith in human nature. You promised you would be good if I brought Maureen here. It wasn't my fault that she wanted to become a ponygirl. Don't worry, she'll be worked hard over the winter. In the spring, she'll be certain to capture a medal again, or she'll rue the day she had a bit put in her mouth."

Jake sensed the tensing of Irving's muscles. He was an unimposing figure under normal circumstances. With his hands behind his back he was even more so. Somehow, though, he managed to cast an aura of moral authority into the room.

"You're a venal, corrupt, soulless bastard, Burnham," he said. "You're time will come. You're too greedy to last very long. Someone, maybe even Borodin here, will knock you off some day, and probably not too far in the future too. You're poisoned by your own corruption. And to think that you are going to hold your own flesh and blood in bondage."

Borodin had had to be brought in on the whole scheme and had been sworn to secrecy. The men he had picked to capture Jake and his men were all rather light in the English department, and were all thoroughly devoted to him. As far as Burnham was concerned, Jake and Irving could say anything that they wanted.

"You don't get it, Irving," Burnham answered. "I don't have a niece anymore. She vanished about eight months ago. All that's left in her place is one of the fastest ponies in the country, a double champion. She'll be running for me for a long time. I can't wait to fuck her."

"Have you ever heard of hubris, Mr. Burnham," Irving interrupted. "Whom the gods would destroy they first make proud. There's a special place in hell for guys like you."

Burnham downed his glass full of scotch and slammed it down on his desk. Releasing Betty's chain, he rose and approached the two bound men.

"I've taken just about as much shit as I can stand from you two assholes. Did you think I would let you run off with the two best ponygirls in the country? Did you think that I would let you destroy this paradise I've made for myself? If there's a hell, there's a special place for stupid fucks like you two."

Burnham had walked around his desk and had approached within a foot of the two men. Betty was watching, horrified. All her hopes of escape had been dashed. She was going to be sold and made into a monster by that Japanese guy Burnham had told her about. Her heart sank and she began to cry. Her mind went back to her enslavement, which had taken place in this very room. Burnham had stripped her naked and pointed a gun at her head. She was given the choice of becoming his slave or receiving a bullet in the brain. He had taken the gun from his desk drawer, the one right in front of her now.

A desperate hope flashed through Betty's head. If the gun was still there, maybe she could turn the tables on Burnham! They could all get away! She didn't know if she could handle a gun with her hands chained to her collar, but it was worth a try. What was he worst that Burnham could do if she failed, kill her? Torture her? If she had known the degradations that Burnham was going to visit upon her body, she would never have chosen to become a slave rather than die. She had kept going the last few months all in the hope that Jake would save her. She didn't care if they visited the worst tortures on her! She had stopped being a slave!

The garishly tattooed woman inched forwards on her knees until her hands were within reach of the handle on the drawer. Burnham was still excoriating Jake and Irving and he took no notice of her. The security men were carefully watching their prisoners. She grabbed the handle and slid the drawer open slowly. There, lying out in the open, waiting for some hand to reach in and give it life was Burnham's pearl handled, gold inlaid Smith and Wesson .45 automatic. Tentatively, she dipped her hands into the drawer, the hands that usually rested prayer-like on her chest. The metal was cold and the gun was heavy. She lifted it out. She knew how to use it, had taken a gun course back in New York many years ago. She slipped off the safety. It made a little click.

Burnham had paused in his tirade. The click of the safety being eased off resounded through the room. All eyes went to the kneeling bird woman. She rose to her feet holding the gun with her two hands pointed at Burnham's heart.

Burnham raised his hands as if to ward off a bullet. "Now, Betty," he said. "You know that you can't do this. My men will drop you in an instant. You'll be dead before you hit the floor. You want to live, don't you?"

"Not like this, I don't, you bastard!" she screamed. All thoughts of escape had faded from her mind. Hearing Burnham's voice using her slave name had set her off. "And I'm not Betty, you fucking scumbag!" she yelled. "I'm Elizabeth!"

When Elizabeth pulled the trigger, all hell broke loose. The first bullet struck Burnham right in the heart. He dropped like a stone. The second shot hit the security man standing behind him. She turned to her right to shoot the startled security chief, Borodin. He had fucked and abused her many times. His piece had been strapped to his hip and he had just cleared his holster when the third bullet passed through his forehead. He got off one shot that struck Jake in the right shoulder, shoving him back against the third security man. Unfortunately for Elizabeth, he had been able to turn his M-16 towards her and gotten off a short burst. Elizabeth's body went flying backwards, a line of angry, red dots emerging on her chest.

When Irving saw that the bird woman had gone down, he turned to the surviving security man and rushed him. He placed his head into the man's chest and drove him until he fell back onto the floor. Irving fell down on top of him.

Jake had fallen when he was struck. The bullet had made a deep hole in his shoulder and blasted out the other side. His adrenalin kicked in. He leaped to his feet and ran towards the remaining security guard. The man had managed to throw Irving off of him and was bringing his M-16 to bear. Jake kicked it away and then landed his boot in the man's face. He fell back. Within an instant, Jake had slammed his boot down on the man's exposed throat. He gave out an anguished, garbled moan, arched his back and died.

Irving and Jake looked at each other. They had to act quickly. The gunshots would surely bring someone to investigate. Without speaking, they brought their backs together and Irving began working the ropes that bound Jake's hands. It was difficult, but after about ten seconds, he had it loose. Jake reached down and picked up one of the cast aside M-16's. Footsteps could be heard coming up the stairs accompanied by men's yells. Jake quickly untied Irving and Irving retrieved the other M-16. They both took a look at the mortal remains of the bird woman. She lay crumpled on the floor, her life's blood seeping all over her colorful chest. There was nothing they could do for her now.

There was a banging at the door. Jake signaled to Irving to go to the door and be ready to open it quickly. When he was in position, Jake nodded and Irving swung the door open. Two of Borodin's security men were standing there looking foolish. Jake dropped them with a short burst.

The two fugitives dashed down the stairs. A security man ran in from the front door but Irving cut him down. They could hear shots coming from outside somewhere.

Once outside, they ran towards the barn. Some of the security men were creeping cautiously from the barracks. Jake sprayed the barracks and they all ducked for cover.

It was a few seconds later that they entered the barn. Curley, Leon and three of Borodin's men were lying on the floor, blood gushing from their wounds. The fourth security guard looked like someone had bashed his head in with a shovel. Tucker was holding the shovel.

"Quick!" Jake shouted. "Get the girls. Me and Irving will hold them off!"

Tucker, blood oozing from a wound to his side, seeing Jake's injury said. "You'll never make it Jake. I'll hitch them up to a troika cart!"

Jake nodded and went outside the barn, crouching at the corner. He felt weak, but was still alert enough to operate the automatic rifle. Two of the security men had gotten enough nerve to charge the barn. They paid for their rashness.

Irving took the other corner in case some of the men tried to get around the barn that way.

Tucker, using all of his bear-like strength began to haul the ponies from their stalls. When he came to Lightning's stall, as he unfastened her bindings, he told her, "I'm an American. I've come to save you. Get up! I've got to hitch you to a cart! One of our men is hurt!

Maddy had lain there for the better part of two days wondering when her torment as the new ponygirl in the barn would begin. The doctor had treated her foot several times and bandaged it well. The sound of the man's voice announcing her rescue took a moment to register. "Rescue? Me? Oh my god!" she exclaimed in her mind. She quickly and unquestioningly rose to her feet. She had heard the gunshots and wondered what was going on. Now she knew.

Tucker then ran to Jackie's stall. The other ponygirls, all mounted in their stalls, were moaning and screeching through their gags, straining at the chains that held them prisoner. Jackie needed no encouragement. Her leg was still injured, but she knew that this was her only chance to get away. When Tucker freed her, she ran to the front of the barn.

Maddy was amazed to see the chocolate colored pony there. "What is going on?" she thought. "Am I going crazy?"

Tucker came running out of the stall area with Czarina, Maureen, behind him. He had told her nothing about the rescue, but was leading her by the ring in her nose. She was trained to obedience and so she followed him willingly.

The troika car was just outside the barn. Tucker led the ponies to it one by one and hooked them up. His experience in caring for his beloved work ponies, Dora and Flora, was serving him well. He had the three hitched up in an instant. He limped back to where Jake was spraying bullets right and left, keeping the bad guys' heads down. He collapsed next to him. The blood had run all the way down his leg and was squishing in his boot.

"I'll take over, Jake!" he said. "You get out of here!"

Jake looked back at him. "No! I'll stay! You and Irving take the girls to the LZ!"

Tucker put his hand on Jake's shoulder. "I'll never make it Jake. I'm hit too bad. You go. Save yourself, save Maddy. It's what we came here to do."

Jake saw that Tucker was finished. Although he was not much better, he knew that Tucker maybe had minutes to live. All the running around and hitching up the ponies had accelerated the bleeding.

"Okay, Tucker," Jake said, handing him the rifle. He tried to think of the right thing to add. Tucker had worked with him a long time. They had been through a lot. Curly and Leon were already lying dead inside the barn. What a fuckup!

But there was nothing he could say. "Goodbye, Tuck," he said solemnly.

Irving was firing away at some men who were trying to outflank them. "Come on!" Jake yelled as he jumped on the seat of the cart. He knew that there was no way he could run a mile with his shoulder wound. The ponies would have to carry him.

Irving tossed off one last burst and then ran towards the cart. He climbed aboard and Jake snapped the reins, "Ya! Ya! Ya!" he yelled.

As if shot from a cannon, the ponygirls jumped to life. The route to the LZ had been carefully planned so that no car or truck could follow them. The path was narrow and passed through a marsh. It would be hard enough to get the cart through it.

Tucker ran towards the trail and took a position from which he could dominate its approaches. He had grabbed one of the other M-16's that had been dropped by the security guards since the one that Jake had given him was almost out of ammunition. He watched the ponycart turn the corner and disappear. He turned back and caught two of the security men rushing him.

While Tucker had been hitching up the ponies, a late model, shiny, black Mercedes had pulled up into the driveway in front of the mansion. Anton Drabik had driven like the devil to get to the Burnham estate. What should have taken him thirteen hours had taken ten and a half. He had tried to leave his estate earlier, but there was still too much confusion, too many orders to give, decisions to make. He got on the road by 8 o'clock. It was now 6:30 and the sun had fled. Darkness was beginning to spread over the estate.

He had heard the shooting as he drove up. He jumped from his car and dove down next to one of Burnham's security men.

"What the fuck is going on!" he yelled.

"They're stealing the ponygirls!" the man answered.

"Lightning!" Drabik thought. They couldn't! They just couldn't!

"What are you waiting for, rush them!" Drabik ordered. The security man just pointed to the four men lying in heaps on the ground in front of them.

"You rush them!" he replied.

Drabik yanked the M-16 from his grasp.

As Irving and Jake dashed away from the barn on the troika cart, Drabik rounded the corner. Tucker had just cut down the two men who were rushing him. Calmly, as if in a trance, Drabik dropped to one knee, leveled the M-16 and shot off three rounds. Tucker's head exploded.

Drabik yelled to the men to get a car so they could pursue the villains, but one of the men told him about the marsh that would have to be traversed.

"Hitch up a ponyteam!" Drabik ordered. The now leaderless men were all to glad to have someone give them direction.

"The yearling team!" he added frantically. The yearlings would be strong enough to carry him and have the advantage of having run together over the last six months.

The two ponies, a blond tailed former German female and a black haired Spaniard, were yanked from their stalls and hitched up quickly to their familiar cart. One of the other men went to mount it, but Drabik shoved him aside.

"I'll get them!" he snarled. The M-16 draped over his shoulder, he held the reins in one hand and gave each pony a fierce crack of the dressage whip. They jumped into action.

* * * * * * * * * * * * * *

Jake and Irving were being hauled at not quite a breakneck speed over the narrow path. Czarina was big enough to drag them anywhere, but speed was not her forte. The other ponies, unused to working in a team, were struggling along, their not quite healed injuries hampering them. If Jake had been able to drive, it would have been one thing. He had gotten plenty of practice taking Tucker's beloved team, Flora and Dora, out for leisurely trots on a regular basis along the shaded pathways of the estate. But Jake had lost a lot of blood and was beginning to get weak. So, it was up to Irving to steer the ponies and he was barely up to the job.

"Crack the whip!" Jake yelled at him, looking back. The firing had stopped, not a good sign. He had expected Tucker to hold out longer.

Irving put aside his qualms about whipping ponygirls. He struck the rear haunches of the three ponies repeatedly, yelling, "Ya! Ya! Ya!" just as he had heard the drivers do.

Lightning groaned at the sharp, familiar sensation that the whip brought, but she was glad for it. Chocolate too, drew inspiration from the fierce fire that bit her rear quarter. She knew that this was her only chance at freedom and needed all the help she could get. Czarina, the mammoth sized super heavyweight, shrugged the pain off. She had no idea what was happening, but she was glad to get out of the barn again to show her stuff. She had heard Irving's voice, the one voice that she had been yearning to hear ever since she had voluntarily given up life as a human female. She had seen his unhappiness with her decision and she wanted him to know that she had no regrets, that she was still grateful to have shucked off all her former insecurities and unhappiness as a woman. Whatever their destination, she sensed Irving's urgency and was giving it her all.

Jake looked at the thick, churning legs of the ponies in front of them. He had to laugh at the irony of them fulfilling their roles as ponies up to the last. There was an incongruous beauty in their forms, an alluring aspect to their total obedience. He realized that, win or lose, it would be the last view of the remarkable creatures of this strange land that he would have and he felt a twinge of sadness for it.

They had progressed the better part of a quarter mile when they hit the swamp that lay across their route of escape. They went on for about twenty yards and the wheels dug deeply into the mud and stopped.

"Christ almighty!" Jake yelled. He turned to look if anyone was following them yet. He knew that it would not take long for the men to figure out that they too could take a ponygirl over this track.

"I'll get out!" Irving yelled. He leapt down from the cart and went to its rear to push. Jake held the reins and with all the strength he could muster, laid several, harsh lines of red across Czarina's back. "Dig in!" he yelled. "Dig in!"

He could see the oversized pony lean into the straps that bound it to the three pony cart. She was in the middle and Lightning and Chocolate were on either side of her. All three ponies strained to pull the cart through the mud.

The going was slow. Jake turned to Irving. "Unhitch them! Leave me behind! You've got to get going!"

The light was fading fast and Martinez was due to land soon. His instructions were to wait fifteen minutes and then take off. If their plans had somehow been delayed, he would be able to come back the next night and the next until they met him at the LZ. But there would be no tomorrow if they didn't meet up with him tonight.

"No! Irving yelled back. "Stay in the cart! We've almost got it!"

The cart began to pick up some movement. The swamp was not big, maybe 150 yards across. They were more than half way there. The going was getting better.

Jake looked back again and saw the silhouette of a pony team, a dark figure driving them, rise and fall over a hill about 300 yards behind them. Some sixth sense told him that it was his nemesis, Anton Drabik.

The cart began to move and Irving ran around the side and hopped back on. He cracked the whip and the three ponygirls snapped into a determined sprint. Jake leaned back and shifted the M-16 that he still carried. He leveled it and began to draw a bead on the next rolling hilltop the ponies behind him would have to cross. The setting sun was behind them and he would get a good shot.

As the ponies and their demonic driver came into view, Jake hesitated. The movements of the troika cart would make his shot uncertain. He might hit the ponies instead of Drabik. He didn't want murder to be his last act in Kalikastan. He had already done enough harm. He pulled the rifle back and shouted to Irving, "Hurry up! We've got company!"

Drabik saw his quarry several hundred yards ahead, not so far ahead as when they started. He took the reins into one hand and brought his rifle to bear. Then he thought twice. What if he hit Lightning? He would be deprived of the fulfillment of his need to feel her life slipping away in his own hands. No, he thought. I'll catch them and kill the Americans. Then he would circle the pony's throat with his hands and squeeze until the life had flowed out of her, ending his torment forever.

Drabik's team had less trouble with the swamp than did the troika. He jumped from the cart right away and let the two practiced ponies pull the lighter cart through the morass. They were out of it quickly and back in the chase.

Over the next half mile, Drabik came closer and closer to the troika cart. Czarina and the two other ponies were doing their best, but their lack of coordination as a team and the injuries to Lightning and Chocolate were telling. Soon, Drabik would be close enough to get off a clean shot at the men, or maybe the heavy set pony in the middle. If she crashed to the ground, it would be all over.

Jake kept glancing nervously back at Drabik's team. Irving was going wild with the whip, urging the ponies to their extreme effort.

Suddenly, out of the northern sky, they heard the unmistakable sound of a helicopter's rotors cutting through the air. It was almost dark now, but there was just enough light so that the pilot would be able to make out the landing zone.

The fugitives were two hundred yards from the LZ when the whirlybird put down. But Drabik was less than that behind them. Were it not for the creeping darkness, the killer would have been able to take them out easily.

When they were thirty yards away from the waiting helicopter, the swirling winds from its blades began to sweep all the loose underbrush from the trail around them, acting as a kind of strange, magical camouflage. They were going to make it!

Maddy and Jackie saw their deliverance waiting before them. They dug fiercely into the ground to climb the small hill where freedom beckoned. Jake was fading fast, teetering on the edge of consciousness. Drabik saw the helicopter and swung the M-16 so that he could get off a desperate shot.

Jake heard Irving shouting something at him. The world was growing foggy. He knew that they needed to unhitch the ponies before they boarded the helicopter and he hoped that somehow Martinez would see their pursuer and take him out. They were within 50 feet of the whirling mechanism. Jake looked up and saw the door to the copter slide open. To his surprise, five armed men jumped out, all wearing the uniforms of the Kalikastani Security Forces. Behind them, he saw the familiar face of his friend, Irkut. They were fucked! Jake passed out.

CHAPTER NINE

It was almost spring in Kalikastan. The wildflowers were struggling through the hard packed earth and here and there shot up the harbingers of purple and green clusters of crocuses or small assemblies of bright yellow daffodils. Jake had his right foot up on the rail of the training ring and was watching his good friend Irkut put a new pony through her paces. The pony had been delivered a few days ago and was rapidly developing its ability to run with its hands bound behind it, its only view of the world that which it could absorb through the tiny holes of her jet black hood.

The hood was a black as her skin and, if you looked quickly, it was difficult to demark where the hood ended and her jet black skin began. She was Kenyan, part of a deal that Burnham had set up before his demise. Jake was continuously surprised at how far Burnham's tentacles had reached in so short a time.

It was mesmerizing to watch the pony scramble around in the small circle. Although the day was cool by any standards, her body was wet with her sweat and glistened in the late afternoon light. Irkut had named the pony Diablo due to its dark hue and fiery spirit. She would be hard to match for their yearling team. Her partner, as yet unchosen, would have to be as feisty and energetic as she or the pair of newly dehumanized ponies would never click.

There had been some talk of a sort of "Tour de Kalika-stan' in June. The ponies would race in timed stages all across the country terminating at the Spring Tournament. It would be a real test of endurance. Diablo looked like a good candidate. Her legs were strong and her back broad. Irkut had had her on the training wheel for the last two hours at a very good pace and she still hadn't slowed down.

Life was leisurely these days for Jake. From time to time he was called in to the mansion to make some decision or other, but essentially, Burnham's corporate empire ran itself as did the slave training center and the ponybarn. Martinez had been put in charge of the construction of the new resort on Lake Novrograd. Irving was busy developing his ponygirl cart design company while keeping his hand in the science game. He was building a new lab about thirty miles north of Dlitski. Kalikastan was a country where you could get anything you wanted for a price. He was working on some cool new stuff using technologies pirated from the US, Western Europe and Japan. He was in partnership with Burnham Industries and, of course, the Kalikastani Government, such as it was.

During the winter, Jake's shoulder had gradually stopped aching from his wound. The slug that had passed through had been as big as an acorn and the bleeding had been stopped just in time to save his miserable life. As he watched the big, black pony continue her rounds, he felt a little twinge in it, a twinge that brought him back to when he woke up in the hospital after the Maddy rescue fiasco.

Jake awoke in a hospital bed. His right arm was hanging in a sling and a large, heavy bandage was on his shoulder. His foot was chained to the bed frame. The room was small. The walls consisted of faded yellow painted cinderblock. There was a small, barred window to the right of the bed. He cursed himself for still being alive and passed out again.

The next few days, while Jake regained his strength, his heart grew heavier and heavier. There was a businesslike, brusque, Russian doctor who refused to answer his questions and a broad bottomed, broad shouldered, ancient nurse who apparently spoke only Russian. She gaily gave him his shots, cleaned his wound and took his temperature, three times a day.

His meals were brought by a slender, black haired slave girl, apparently condemned to silence. She would glide into the room soundlessly, give him a bow and drop his tray on his lap. She had small, pointed breasts and a coiled snake tattooed on her belly. Her name was Irina, as Jake detected from the writing on her upper chest. She never looked him in the eye or smiled. Jake wondered what kind of a place he was being kept in.

Most of the time, Jake was forced to lie alone in the primitive room, thinking about how he had let everyone down. He mourned for Leon and Curley. Tucker too. He thought of Madeline, now condemned to a lifetime of torment, as well as Jackie. The last time he had seen her as a free woman had been in Chicago six months before. They had fucked like lemmings. He remembered her unpretentious laugh, the way she freely gave herself. There was Mary Ellen too, and her lesbian teammates who had run the Jersey slaving operation. He didn't feel as bad for her and her girls as the others. Their fate, dehumanized and slated for training as a six in hand, was actually somewhat ironi-cally just.

If there was true justice though, he mooned repeatedly, he would be dead. Why they had let him live, he didn't know. Maybe they were waiting until he was all better before applying the most heinous tortures they could devise on his flesh. Now, he thought, that would be justice.

The only good thing was the death of the billionaire, Michael Burnham. If it weren't for his greed and inner corruption, Maddy and Jackie would be free women, Leon, Curley and Tucker would be alive, and the slaving operation in the States, the same one that had brought Maddy to Kalikastan in the first place, would be shut down. He imagined that Burnham used some of his new mob connections to take over the place. Now, for the foreseeable future, young girls all over the United States would continue to lose their freedom and everything that was worthwhile to them. Hundreds more would take the one way trip in a silver canister to Kalikastan.

It was too bad about Betty. When he thought of the monster that Burnham had made of her and how her courage had been rewarded with death, his eyes began to tear and he turned his head to the wall.

On the third day of his isolation, someone finally came in to see him. He remembered him at once. He was the security apparatchik who Jake had met many months ago when he and Burnham were trying to establish their bona fides as slavers and general ne'er-do-wells. There had been a big party in the private room of a restaurant in Dlitski. It was Burnham's first real exposure to the moral cesspool that was Kalikastan. Jake guessed that he could trace Burnham's slide into decadence from that night. Six lovely, naked slave girls had danced for their amusement and then sucked all their cocks.

But what was he talking about? It wasn't like he was Francis of Assisi. Burnham had been right at their final confrontation. He was the one who had thought of the takeover of the Jersey slaving operation, of worming their way into Kalikastan, of becoming ponygirl owners so that, in the guise of building up their stock, Jake could tour the inner portions of the country in search of Maddy. He had used dozens and dozens of slave girls, whipped some. Up to the last minute, he had succumbed to his untrammeled lusts by getting a farewell blowjob from his slave, Dana, and then callously locked her back up in her cage.

Vladimir Boretski stood by the foot of Jake's bed, a killer's look in his eyes. He was wearing a cheap, rumpled, black suit, a white shirt and a narrow, featureless tie. His handgun made a little bulge under his shoulder.

When Jake had first met Boretski, he had thought about how similar they were. They were both no nonsense men, men of violence, when called for, men of business when convenient or necessary. He was the one to tell Jake that Burnham's bid to purchase an estate had been approved by the National Commission.

Boretski lit a cigarette, a filterless, domestic brand, and handed it to Jake. Jake took it and sucked a cloud of smoke into his lungs. When he released it, the room turned grey. Boretski lit one for himself.

"You have made a hash of things, comrade," he intoned. His voice was raspy and his English heavily accented. He was small and wiry, like Jake, and, like Jake, he carried himself like someone who knew well his own formidability. He was older than Jake, maybe 45 or so. His grayish hair had been shaved down to a crew cut.

Jake shrugged in response. He knew that Boretski wasn't looking for an explanation or excuses. And he certainly wasn't expecting Jake to plead for his life. Jake just waited for the man to expose the purpose of his visit.

There was no ashtray. There was a potted plant, brown and scraggly from lack of sunlight and water, on the bedside table. It sat atop a small, dirty, round dish meant to capture the escaping moisture that never came. Boretski took the plant off of the dish and set the dish down on Jake's bed. Jake flicked his ash into it. Boretski followed suit.

"But you are a lucky motherfucker," Boretski finally added. "It seems that you have some continued usefulness for the time being. Are you interested? If you say 'yes', all will be explained for you in a little while. If you say 'no' then, well, I will shoot you before I leave, after I finish my smoke."

Jake took a deep drag on his cigarette. Maybe he should let them finish him off. A bullet to the brain was not a bad way to go. What did he have to live for, anyway? Then he thought of Tanya. Beautiful, joyful, Tanya. If living meant that he could spend even just one more night with her, maybe it would be worth it. It was worth, at least, hearing out the terms of the chance he was being given to live.

There was a set of ankle shackles in the small room that had been used by the nurse when she took Jake from his bed to perform his necessaries. Boretski retrieved them and, after releasing the chain that held his ankle to the bed, snapped them on Jake's legs. Jake had a reputation of a guy who managed to get out of some pretty bad scrapes. Boretski was a professional and there was no way he would take a chance that Jake might be inclined to turn the tables on him.

Jake had no such intention. Crushing out the tiny, remaining stub of his cigarette, he docilely let his feet fall to the floor and stood from the bed. He was still a little weak from loss of blood and he had to sit still for a moment until his head cleared. He slid his feet into the little, canvas slippers that had been provided and gave Boretski the signal that he was ready. He was dressed in a long hospital gown, more like a sheath. He was a pitiable sight. He hadn't shaved for days, his face was gaunt from his lack of appetite and the struggle to recover from his injury. He had even started to stoop a little as the weight of his failures pressed down on him.

The room in which he had been kept prisoner was stark, but the hallway was somewhat more pleasant. It was covered with a thick, commercial carpet of burnt orange. The walls, still of the same cinderblock of his cell, were painted a bright blue and had various happy prints of flowers, beautiful landscapes and cute little animals on the walls. Several nurses passed them on their trek down the hall, a couple of them with naked and bound slave girls in tow. While Jake's door had been padlocked and was steel encased, the doors to the other rooms were open and visiting men and women were coming in and out of the rooms.

The chains around his ankles made little clinking sounds as he shuffled along. The chain was only about 18" in length and his gait was considerably slower than the passing pedestrians. The men and women looked at him as if he were some kind of prehistoric discovery, unfrozen from the icy north. Boretski just kept walking slowly and blithely at his side.

When they reached the end of the corridor, Boretski pushed the button for the elevator. It opened a few moments later. A male and female couple stepped out. Three more people had gathered behind Jake and his warder as they waited for the silver doors of the lift to open. Before Jake and Boretski got in, the Russian turned and flashed a badge at the people behind them. He didn't have to say anything. A cloud passed over their faces and they all stepped back. Jake and Boretski rode the elevator to the top floor all alone.

When the doors opened, the contrast between the somewhat barracks like atmosphere of the ground floor and the sumptuous décor of the penthouse level could not have been greater. There was a light green, deep pile, wall to wall carpet. The walls were covered with a lavish green, gold and blue wallpaper. Instead of the commercial type lighting that lined the ceiling in the lower hallway, brass and crystal chandeliers hung down every twenty or so feet down the expansive hallway.

Right outside the elevator doors was a desk. A well dressed, sophisticated woman, late thirties, blond, with a nice figure, sat behind it. She smiled at Boretski and waved him and Jake through. A man who was undoubtedly a security guard, probably one of Boretski's crew, stood nearby the desk, a holstered, automatic pistol on his belt. He was dressed in black jeans and a black t-shirt. Jake guessed that he had been making time with the receptionist and had paused in his hopeful attentions to the attractive lady only because he had heard the elevator coming. When he saw Boretski, he kind of stiffened. A nod from Boretski put him back at ease.

Jake baby-stepped his way down the hallway. He passed several elegantly furnished hospital rooms, most of them empty. One had an older man in the bed, a security guard sitting outside his door. An elderly lady, maybe in her late sixties, was standing near the door with tears in her eyes. It looked to Jake like one of the masters of this strange version of hell was about to go meet his maker. He wondered what God would think about all this.

They stopped before the door to a conference room. Boretski opened the door and let Jake proceed him in.

There was a large, finely polished, dark oak table in the middle of the room. It was surrounded by finely upholstered, gold chairs. The walls were covered with a dark brown, almost ebony wallpaper. A large chandelier hung over the table. Sitting at the table was a well dressed man. He had short, wavy, salt and pepper hair. His suit was soft and elegant and clearly especially tailored for his frame. There was a small, glass carafe in front of him with a clear liquid in it. Three fine, short, crystal glasses were on the table next to it.

The man smiled at Jake as he entered the room. He was smoking a gold tipped, filter cigarette and the room seemed a little hazy. He crushed the cigarette out in a dinner plate sized, ceramic ashtray in front of him. Jake remembered him well. Oscar Kasperov, President of the National Commission. He had met him at Burnham's big party early in the summer. Jake was surprised that whatever they were going to proffer to him as a condition of keeping him alive could not be sent via a message boy. Things were looking up.

"Mr. Barnes," Kasperov greeted him. "Sit down and have a drink. We need to talk."

The man's voice was a smooth as butter. He had a smile that was warm and friendly, but his eyes were as cold as death. He pointed to a chair next to him and Jake plopped himself down in it. Boretski kept standing by the door. Jake wasn't sure he should have a drink. Just walking down the hall had exhausted him. "I must have lost a lot of blood," he thought.

Kasperov poured the clear liquid into two of the glasses and then proffered one to Jake. His hand shaking, Jake reached out for it. "What the hell," he thought. They gave each other a little nod and shot the liquor back. Vodka, at least 125 proof. A chill ran down Jake's spine even as his chest burned. It was primo stuff. He set his glass back down on the hardwood table.

"So what's on your mind," he said with a little less confidence than he intended.

"I'm sure that I don't have to tell you," Kasperov began, "that you have committed a capital crime by trying to take a ponygirl out of the country. And to be responsible for the death of one of our leading citizens, that was very bad too. By all rights, you should be moldering in a grave somewhere after having spent twenty or so hours learning what pain really is."

"Sure," was all Jake could say in response. His head was swimming.

"Mr. Burnham's death has left us quite a dilemma," Kasperov continued. "He was at the center of a great deal of what we'll call for the moment 'economic activity'. His death could mean the loss of hundreds of millions of dollars to us. The contacts that he made internationally, not to mention the pipeline project he brought us, were all dependant on the fact that he was someone whom all parties could trust. He was virtually irreplaceable."

"I'm sorry about all that," Jake returned. "It wasn't in the plan."

"No," Kasperov agreed. "I would guess that it wasn't. But you know what they say about best laid plans."

Kasperov's English was perfect. He looked like a guy who never broke into a sweat. Jake watched him as he retrieved another gold tipped cigarette from his pack. He proffered one to Jake. Jake waived him off.

"How about another shot?" he asked. The booze was making him woozy, but he felt like he needed some fortification. Kasperov smiled. He poured two more glasses and the men threw them back quickly. Jake felt his adrenaline jumping into gear.

"The loss of Mr. Burnham's contacts is only half the problem." Kasperov continued. "The fact is that he was the sole stockholder of Burnham Enterprises whose credit is underwriting the entire pipeline project. With his death, the backers have become very nervous. Several of the international banks are threatening to call in their notes. Burnham Industries is without a leader and the person who is the sole heir to the Burnham empire was kidnapped eight months ago on a country road in the southern United States and has not been heard from since."

Jake had realized that they would make the connection between Maddy and Burnham without too much trouble once they really started looking. He wondered, too, how much Irving had told them. Irving was a steadfast co-conspirator, but Jake doubted that he could stand up long under the kind of pain these men were capable of inflicting. Probably nobody could.

"And so, you see, unless stability is brought to Burnham Enterprises as soon as possible, the pipeline project will be cancelled. Unfortunately, one of the richest women in the world is also a two time ponygirl champion. Do you see the problems that you've caused us?"

Jake was emboldened by the effects of the vodka. "I certainly do," he answered.

At that moment, there was a knock on the door to the conference room. Jake, being the world wise detective that he was, had deduced that a third person was to join their conference. He had been wondering who it would be.

"Come in," Kasperov called out loudly. The door opened slowly. In walked Anton Drabik.

If there had been gasoline in the room, it would have exploded. Sparks flew between the two similar yet drastically opposed men. Jake felt vulnerable with his arm in a sling. He looked to Kasperov.

"Relax, Mr. Barnes. You are under my protection. Mr. Drabik is here to make sure that all the issues concerning the ponygirl Lightning are settled." He pointed to a chair to his right and Drabik sank into it uneasily. Jake could see the reciprocal hatred boiling up in is eyes.

"Mr. Drabik has much to answer for himself," Kasperov said. "You see, he knew the former identity of Lightning for many months and about the plot to take her from the country. He should have revealed it to us immediately. Instead, he kept it under his hat, as you Americans like to say. He wanted to use his information as a trump card should Lighting lose the claiming race, as she did. His malfeasance almost permitted the ponygirl Lightning, and two others, to escape. There was some talk in the Commission of having him shot, but we don't want to cause a power vacuum in the former Grobgy organization."

Jake was startled by the news. He hadn't heard of Grobgy's demise, but then, no one had been telling him much of anything over her last few days. Kasperov saw his surprise.

"Yes, Mr. Drabik now heads that organization with the National Commission's blessing. But if he is to be a responsible member of our circle, he must play by the rules. I understand that he has something that belongs to you."

At this, Jake sprang to attention. There was only on 'thing' that he could have. Klara! Klara was alive! He didn't believe it. He had often mourned for her loss. She had been a devoted slave and he had felt guilty that she had been seized, and he thought, tortured and killed, to get at him.

"Where is she?" Jake demanded.

Kasperov waived Jake down. His voice was soothing and authoritative.

"She's being taken care of. She was not in very good condition when she was turned over to us. She will get well again, I am assured, but it will take some time. You can see her later."

Jake's hand circled around the small crystal glass he had drunk from. He needed to hold on to something. He was glad that Klara was alive, but he seethed with anger at what Drabik had probably put her through. He cursed himself too for not protecting her.

"Right now, we are going to all have a drink together to signify that bygones will be bygones. Comrade Drabik here will forget that you managed to take his favorite ponygirl away from him and you, Jake, will forget what Anton did to your favorite slave girl. She is just a slave girl after all."

Just a slave girl after all. That was a reality that Jake would have to face were he to accept whatever deal the Commission was going to offer him. He had promised himself that he would hear the offer out and he would stick to his promise. That didn't mean that he would take it.

But if he didn't, what would happen to Klara? Would they go through all the trouble of rehabilitating her if he wasn't around? No, it was more likely that they would throw her on the dung heap. It was just one more reason to keep on living.

Kasperov poured three shots. Jake had released his glass and took it back once it was filled. Drabik picked up his. The two men glared at each other. Kasperov picked up his drink.

"If there is any trouble between you two after today," Kasperov said emphatically, "one or both of you will pay the price, no matter what the consequences. Do you both understand?"

Drabik's hand clutched the glass as if it were the throat of his adversary. His face was fraught with anger. He looked at Kasperov and then back at Jake. "Da!" he spat out.

Jake had been returning the man's fiery gaze. He wanted to spit in the evil man's face. He thought of Tanya, and he restrained himself. If he didn't go along, he would never see her again. And then there was Jackie, and Maddy too. As long as he was alive, there was the chance that he could still save them. If he were dead, there would be no chance at all. "I understand," he hissed towards the killer. "Now, drink up," Kasperov said. All three men swallowed the liquor in one gulp.

"Now that we're all friends, we can move on to the next issue." There was a telephone on the wall behind Kasperov and he leaned back and picked up the receiver. He hit three buttons and a man's voice came on. "You can send her in now," he said.

There was silence in the room while the men waited for Kasperov's new guest to arrive. Jake could not help imagining Drabik with a bullet hole in his head. Drabik did the same for him.

A few moments later, the door to the conference room opened again. All eyes turned towards it. It was a woman. She was covered head to foot in a dark blue, hooded robe. There was a cloth wrapped around her face, giving the outfit the appearance of a burkha. She walked hesitatingly into the room. Her hands hung uselessly at her sides. The man who had escorted her into the room led her to a chair and, speaking softly to her, instructed her to sit. The woman looked down on the chair as if it were some strange object and then hesitatingly lowered herself into it. She looked at the men across the table from her for a moment and then her eyes were cast downwards.

"Gentlemen," Kasperov announced somewhat regally, "may I introduce you to one of the richest young women in the world, Madeline Burnham."

Jake looked at her with shock. The woman he had been chasing down, who he had schemed to rescue, for whom Curley, Leon and Tucker had given their lives was right in front of him. She was stripped of her ponygirl regalia. She seemed frail, quite unlike the noble creature who had won a gold medal in the Fall Tournament less than a week ago. Jake looked over at Drabik. He was staring at her with hungry eyes. It was then that he understood why Drabik had come to the Burnham estate on the day of their foiled escape attempt. He was in love with her! Jake almost laughed.

Drabik was trembling. Here was the object of his obsession right before him. She was within a yard or two of where he sat, but she might as well have been a thousand miles away. He clamped his hands into fists in frustrated rage.

"The National Commission has decided that, in this one instance, we will make an exception to the ironclad rule that once a ponygirl, always a ponygirl," Kasperov declared. "Ms. Burnham will be permitted to take possession of her fortune with some limitations. We have spoken to the American Ambassador and he will authen-ticate the necessary documents so that Michael Burnham's Will can be admitted to probate in New York. Ms. Burnham will execute an irrevocable power of attorney allowing her financial empire to be, let's say, managed by others. This is where you come in, Jake."

"Me?" Jake asked, perplexed. "What am I supposed to do?"

"It is fortunate for you that you are in a position to satisfy several of our needs. Someone whom Ms. Burnham trusts will become the guardian of her person and her property. She is to remain in Kalikastan, although she will be free to live as a person for so long as she cooperates. The Commission gave her her choice: you, Jake, or Anton here. At first she was determined to place herself into Anton's hands. It seems that she reciprocated his affections for her. However, once she learned of Anton's concealment of her identity and apparent intent to keep her as a ponygirl in spite of that knowledge, she changed her mind. She chose you, Jake. You will be Ms. Burnham's new guardian."

Jake stared at the frail young woman before him. What would he do with her? He knew that she was undoubtedly terribly scarred from her experiences. She would need therapy, kindness, patience. She would still be a prisoner, but she would have a gilded cage.

Kasperov resumed his exposition of Jake's new life.

"That is one need that you will satisfy. The American Ambassador has indicated that he will certify annually Ms. Burnham's well being so that her control, or rather, her designee's right to manage her affairs will be unquestioned in the West. The other need that you will satisfy is this, Jake. Mr. Burnham's former underworld connections have insisted on a middleman for our relationships, someone neutral, someone they can trust. It seems that you have quite a reputation. The American Italian organizations proposed you and the others, based on their recommendations, accepted. You will be sitting on top of one of the greatest fortunes in the world, Jake. You will be accepted as a non-voting member of the National

Commission. You will just have one limitation. You too are forbidden to ever leave Kalikastan. Maybe later, after your absolute loyalty is assured, after you have become more accustomed to and accepting of our ways, maybe we can talk then. Until that time, however, you will conduct your business from here."

Jake was dumfounded. In a flash, Kasperov had made him the functional equivalent of a billionaire. The trade off would be his soul. He could never assuage his guilt at the things that he did, the women who he played a role in bringing to this dark country. Deep inside, he knew that he should say no. But then he thought of Tanya. He wanted her so badly, he could taste it. He had spent decades alone, sealed within himself. He had finally found someone he could love. He didn't know what to do.

"What about Jackie?" Jake asked. "What will become of her?"

"I'm afraid that I'm not familiar with any Jackie, Jake," Kasperov answered. "I do know a ponygirl named *Shoko-ladniy*. Right now she is being housed in a ponybarn not far from here. She will, of course, remain the property of Burnham Enterprises and part of the assets that you will be responsible for. But if anyone ever got the thought that she could be human again, they would pay a terrible price."

Jake's heart sank. "Poor Jackie," he thought. His unhappiness at his failure to save her rose up in his belly like bile. Then a thought occurred to him. As long as he was alive, there was always the chance that he could figure out a way, with or without the Commission's permission, to save her from her fate. If he refused Kasperov's deal, he would be dead and Jackie would have no hope of recovering her humanity. He had to stay alive! He had to accept Kasperov's offer! And Maddy, too. He was the only person who would ever help her escape from Kalikastan. It might not be right away, they would be watched like hawks at the beginning. But later, when the monitoring of them would be relaxed, then he would get his chance to fulfill his pledge.

"I'll only do it if Maddy asks me to," he replied. "I won't be her jailer unless it's with her consent."

"She has already consented," Kasperov said.

"I need to hear it from her," was Jake's retort. "She has to tell me that she wants it."

All three men looked at the frail, young woman. She had been sitting docilely at the round table on the opposite side from them while her future was being bandied about. She became alert now. A muted voice, one unused to speech, emerged from behind the cloth that covered her face. "Please, Jake, please take care of me," she said plaintively, her voice little more than a whisper. "You're the only one I can trust."

"Madeline!" Drabik interjected. "Please! Please choose me! I need you! I will never do anything to harm you! I promise!"

The desperation in the killer's voice was piteous. Jake looked at him with contempt, but remained silent. Maddy spoke again, her voice barely audible.

"No." she said. "You don't love me. You love a ponygirl named Lightning. Lightning no longer exists. I could never have faith in someone who wanted me to remain a beast. It was bad enough that my uncle, my own uncle...." She burst into tears. She lay her head down on the table, covered it with her thin, emaciated arms and cried like a baby. The men watched her silently, powerless to assuage her grief.

Finally, Kasperov spoke. "You have your answer, Jake, as well as you Anton. It will be as the Commission has decided. And Anton," he said gravely, "our decision is final. If any harm comes to Jake or Ms. Burnham we will hold you personally responsible. You now control a powerful organization, but all the other clans will act as one to destroy you. Do you understand?"

Grimly, Anton Drabik conceded defeat. It was not something that he was used to. Suddenly, his rage overcame him. He swept the carafe of vodka and the three glasses off of the conference table and jumped to his feet. They clattered to the floor with a crash. He cast a bitter, hateful look first at Jake and then at Kasperov. Then he turned and stormed from the room.

Jake spent a few more days in the clinic. His room was changed to one on the penthouse floor, next to the room where Maddy was recuperating. The service improved as well, with youthful, pleasant, nubile nurses and more accommodating slave girls. He spent some time every day with Maddy. She remained dressed in her body covering robe and kept her face shielded from him at all times. She was understandably morose and depressed about her recent past and the limitations on her future. Jake had expected her to show, at least, some joy at the fact of her liberation from the life of a ponygirl, but he was disappointed.

He also went and visited Klara, who was being kept, as befitted a slave girl, in one of the rooms reserved for them in the basement. She was, at first, overjoyed to see him. She was thin and covered with scars from her ordeal. The doctor assured Jake that they would fade with time. After her initial expression of happiness at being reunited with him, she began to cry inconsolably over what she saw as her betrayal of him to Drabik. She had told him everything she knew after a fierce session of abuse. Jake tried to tell her that virtually anyone would have given up anything they could under such circumstances, but this did not seem to comfort her.

When they arrived at the estate, the three of them traveling in Burnham's luxurious caravan, Jake had Maddy installed in the carriage house which had served as his headquarters. Over the weeks that followed, she very rarely left it, and that only to wander aimlessly about the estate, covered from head to foot, for an hour or so and then returning to her sanctuary. Jake tried to get her interested in something that would help get her mind off her past, helping with the running of the mansion, taking enjoyment from the vast bevy of slave girls that inhabited the estate, trips to Dlitski, but nothing availed.

Jake was initially very busy. He needed to get a handle on the vast empire that was Burnham Industries and the extensive underworld connections and deals that Burnham had had going. Eventually, he handed the everyday running of the legitimate aspects to Burnham's former second in command, reserving to himself any major decisions and getting daily briefings on everything else. The more sinister aspects of the web that Burnham had woven, he handled personally.

In between his work, he availed himself of the many diversions of being the virtual owner of dozens of slave girls, not counting the newly arrived young women undergoing training in the slave center. He would go there from time to time to sample one of the fresh recruits, especially enjoying their frightened, nervous aspects, the way their lips trembled when he ordered them to sink to their knees to service his cock, or how they moaned with unhappiness when he sank his thick, stiffened wand into them.

The ponygirls all left for winter quarters about a week after he returned to the estate, Chocolate among them. He was continuously unhappy with his failure to free her, but was philosophical about it. Unlike the other unhappy ponygirls, she had known the risk that she was taking. He had warned her that he might not be able to reverse her dehumanization. Not that he had given up hope of eventually saving her. He just knew that it would not be sometime in the foreseeable future. He had not used her or said anything to her since he came back from the clinic. He didn't want to give her any false hope. It was better that she accommodate herself to her status as a beast, otherwise she might fall afoul of the men who ruled and used her.

Drabik had not lasted long as the ruler of the Grobgy empire. He grew increasingly irrational and started several deadly disputes with other criminal clans in the country. It did not take long for the National Commission to authorize his demise. Jake took the news with bitter satisfaction. Another who was not unhappy about his downfall was his beautiful, Italian slave girl, Antonia. She spent several weeks afterwards as a barracks girl, but then was sold to a rather kindly master who didn't abuse her so often.

It didn't take long for Jake to resume his friendship with Irkut. The slight ponygirl trainer was apologetic at his intervention in the plot to save Maddy, but unrepentant. Jake understood his motives and accepted them. He kept Irkut on as head trainer.

Tanya, at first, came often to the estate and they spent many hours in bed either alone or with one of the delectable slave girls. As suggested by Tanya's mother, they had an early January wedding attended by all the fine notables of the country. The wedding night was a reprise of his evening with the four blond beauties and he was given to understand that he was, in reality, getting married to all of them.

A few weeks after the wedding, Jake went with Tanya to Khalid Rashid's slave market to pick out her show ponies. As usual, Khalid had just what they were looking for. He presented them with two slender, hooded, black haired Portuguese ponies which had been newly converted with Tanya in mind. They had cute, little apple sized breasts. Their bellies were flat and their hips narrow. Their thighs were lithe and well toned. They could have been twins as far as anyone could tell from their bodies' physical characteristics.

Khalid had the ponies demonstrate their grace by a few turns around the courtyard of his facility. They were a delight to watch. Tanya inspected them closely, nonetheless. She felt their breasts and thighs, looked into their mouths. The unhappy, newly minted ponies whined and cried while they were handled, a good omen of their susceptibility to training as their ability to emote would be an important attribute as they learned to perform their routines with grace. She was pleased with their respon-siveness, stroking and probing their newly shaven love lips until they sighed and moaned with lust. This was of paramount importance for their proper training hinged on their development of a dependence on their sexual use.

Tanya was well satisfied. She had initially intended to secure a pair of black beauties to train, but these two were so delicious that she jumped at the opportunity to acquire them. Khalid gave her a deep discount due to her relationship with Jake and Burnham Industries with which Khalid was in partnership in several endeavors. When all the arrangements were made, and before the ponies were loaded into the double wide pony van for transportation to the training facility that Tanya intended to use, she insisted that Jake break them in right on the spot. Khalid had them bend over a rail where Jake fucked first one, and then the other.

After that, Tanya was usually too preoccupied with her ponies to spend much time at the estate. Her sisters, Lada and Zoya, as well as Dr. Svetlana Kevsky more than adequately made up for her absence. Lada stayed for two weeks alternating between sucking Jake's cock and playing with the slave girls. When Dr. Kevsky left after her visit, she took with her Jake's personal slave girl, Dana. Jake was somewhat disconcerted to see the beautiful, black haired American slave girl scrunched up in one of Dr. Kevsky's tiny cages. She looked out at Jake dolefully. On the other hand, he looked forward to getting her back with her occasional surliness removed and her skills brought up a couple of notches.

He had kept Tucker's beloved ponies, Dora and Flora around just to make sure that they were properly treated and in Tucker's memory. When conditions permitted, he had them hitched up and took them for pleasant rides along the snowy paths in the nearby woods. No provision needed to be made for their nakedness as long as he didn't keep them out for too long or didn't leave them standing, The heat of their workout was more than adequate to keep them warm and their boots were high and heavy enough to deal with the snow. Jake had given the ponybarn staff strict instructions that the ponies never be whipped and that they be fucked at least twice a day with provision for them to pleasure each other on a regular basis. It was the least that he could do for Tucker.

Czarina, the former Maureen, also stayed through the long winter months. She was used to pull a plow to clear the pathways of the estate whenever it snowed which was almost daily for a while. When the weather was good, she trained by hauling a sled loaded with bricks along the snow covered roads.

Klara proved to be an intractable problem. She was all right when not in Jake's actual presence, performing light duties around the mansion, helping the other slave girls with their grooming. It was when she saw Jake that she started to fall apart. She would begin with a little sniffle and proceed ineluctably to all out tears. Something had to be done.

In late November, after consultation with Tanya, Jake brought her on a trip with him to the capital. The madam of the house that he brought her to had a reputation for relatively lenient treatment of her charges. Klara cried inconsolably while the madam inspected her, feeling her thighs, weighing her firm, heavy breasts, testing her responsiveness. Her lips trembled when the whore mistress removed her shield gag so that she could examine her face. Most of the scars on her body had healed and she had filled out some from her gaunt appearance when she had been returned to him. The unhappy girl, Jake could see, was terribly tempted to beg and plead that she not be sold, but her slave discipline held her in check.

"She looks fine," the madam told Jake. "We'll take good care of her, I promise." She called one of her slave stewards into the room.

"Alexi, please take Klara downstairs and give her ten strokes with the number 2 cane so that you can become well acquainted. After that, change her disks and then give her a nice bath and something to eat. I'll sample her after dinner."

Jake felt a pang of pity for the sweet girl, but, as he watched her being led away, her chest still heaving from tears, he knew that he had done the right thing.

Maddy was a whole other question. Her depression only seemed to get worse as time went on. Jake was at a loss for what to do. Her melancholia was contagious and several of the slave girls who served her had to be severely whipped to snap themselves out of the funk they fell into after being in her presence.

It was Irkut who convinced Jake. Maddy quailed when she saw the men enter her bedroom in the carriage house carrying the implements of subjugation, a ponycollar and hood and a pair of black ponyboots. She gave them quite a struggle as they shaved her head and loins in preparation for her renewed dehumanization.

Jake had thought it proper that as her guardian and soon to be new master to be present. Maddy looked at him imploringly. "Please, Jake, please!" she screamed as the men manhandled her. "Please don't do this! Please don't make me a ponygirl, please! I couldn't stand it! I'll do anything you want! Anything! Please! Please!"

When her head was properly prepared, her entreaties were silenced by application of a gag. A black ponygirl hood was pulled over her head. Irkut ordered his men to lay her down on the floor on her back and to hold her legs spread wide. Jake, as her new owner, needed to establish his mastery over her. He was careful to make sure that she was properly prepared for his prick by mouthing her pussy until she began to moan and sigh with unwanted pleasure. When he entered her, she gave out a piteous groan. Nonetheless, she soon responded to the sawing of his thick cock. Jake waited until she had climaxed twice before expelling his spume into her, groaning his own pleasure loudly into the small room.

Irkut's men had to practically drag her from the room. Her knees sagged and her body went limp. As they left, Irkut told Jake, "Give me a week or so and she'll be fine."

It was a week and a day later that Lightning was loaded on a pony trailer for her trip to her winter quarters. Jake had come down to see her off. Before they loaded her into the van, Irkut had ordered the naked, buxom pony to her knees with a snap of his fingers. Jake opened his fly and took out his cock. The subservient pony took it into her mouth without hesitation.

Her mouth was hot and her tongue coiled around his cock like a serpent. She took her time in pleasuring him. Jake moaned as his mind received the steady, lust driving waves of pleasure that she brought him. He rested his hands on her black clad head for balance as he swooned with delight. The pony's enthusiasm for her task surprised him. He could hear her giving out pleased moans of her own as her lips rode up and down his crank, held tightly against the soft yet firm flesh. Twice, when he was about to come, she slowed her efforts to prolong his ecstatic enjoyment of her efforts. She circled the knob on the end of his prick with her lips, ran her tongue along the tender underside and then resumed her obeisance to his stiff shaft.

When Jake came, he growled his pleasure, much to the amusement of the attending grooms and stable hands. Lightning made sure that she had received all of his discharge, suckling at his cock's end until she had coaxed out the last drop.

When she pulled back her head from her task, Jake took a look at her face. He could not discern anything about her emotional state from looking there since the thin, black hood obscured all but the outline of her features. But as her gag was reinstalled by Irkut, he thought that he detected a slight rise in her posture, a straightening of her spine, denoting her pride and satisfaction at performing her task well. Maybe it was his imagination, maybe not.

The air was cold and it was a long ride to Dlitski. Because of the subzero temperatures at night, the trailer had a small heater installed so that the pony would not freeze. Jake watched as a blanket was lowered over the back, sealing Lightning inside to protect her from the wind. He watched the trailer depart.

Maybe Burnham had been right, he thought. There was no more Madeline Burnham. She had disappeared the moment that a ponygirl collar was closed around her neck and a hood pulled over her face. Her humanness had dissipated into the air leaving only a ponygirl behind and it could not be recovered. Irkut had told him that, "once a ponygirl, always a ponygirl." It seemed that he was right.

He saw both Lightning and Chocolate several times during his trips to Dlitski over the winter. It snowed heavily and often, but during the lulls he was able to get through by using one of the estate's four wheel drive SUV's. The building that housed the ponies during the winter, one of several in the Dlitski area, was as big as a city block. There were stables for 250 ponies and most of them were filled. It had two training rings, each with a circumference of about 100 yards where the ponies were exercised daily. The former Mary Ellen and her five 'sisters' were there and Jake watched them being taught the rudiments of working as a six pony team. As he had suspected all along, Mary Ellen's breasts were a wonder to behold, round and firm and bigger than cantaloupes. They looked especially pleasing covered by the fierce red stripes left there by her trainers' whips. The former slavers, after being tattooed and ringed, had been brought directly to the winter quarters from the slave reception center run by Khalid Rashini. Jake looked forward to the time when he would be granted his rights to first use of them when delivered to the estate in the early spring.

Jake was careful not to let his presence at the winter ponybarn be known to either Lightning or Chocolate. He watched them train from the stands that surrounded the ring. He did, on his first visit, seek out Chocolate's stall. One of the stable hands had to give him directions.

When he entered the stall, the tall, shapely brown skinned pony was mounted against the bar that ran across it, her ankles spread wide and affixed to rings in the floor and her nose ring tautly connected to a hook in the wall in front of her. Her posture was slightly bent forwards so that her twin orifices were easily available for use.

Jake eased his hardened prick into her smaller, rear hole. The pony sighed as he entered her. He took hold of her heavy breasts and caressed them, making her squirm and begin to pant. He fucked her slowly. He wanted her to come first. He was sure that she had no idea who was fucking her, unless she detected his presence by the feel of his hands or the heaviness of his breath. Her rear hole was pliant and welcoming. Its heat made him shiver with pleasure. When he sensed that the pony was nearing her crisis, he removed his hands from her now hard, blood filled breasts and took hold of her wide hips to give him leverage for the final approach to her orgasm.

Chocolate moaned and squirmed as he was fucking her. When her orgasm began, her body shook and her knees sagged. She emitted a long, deep moan and shook her head, rattling the chain that connected her to the stall wall and causing the championship medal that she wore on her collar to tingle. Jake came too. As his cock throbbed and spurted within her, he drew his body tightly against her back so that he could feel her heat through his shirt.

When he was finished, Jake washed himself in the small sink at the side of the stall. Before he left, he gave Chocolate's rump a solid pat. "I'm sorry, Jackie," he thought. "But a ponygirl you are and a ponygirl you'll stay. See you in the spring."

Now, as Jake stood watching the Kenyan pony go through her paces, he realized that he was anxious for the return of the pony herd. The winter had been harsh and the ponybarn and its environs too long silent. Irkut had made some new acquisitions and he planned to move last fall's yearlings to the four pony brougham and graduating two of those four ponies to the six pony team. The two that he retired Jake sold to Irkut's friend who ran the milk pony tent. Jake had had some talks with him about establishing a permanent facility close to Dlitski where a major market could be found for ponymilk.

The late afternoon sun went behind a cloud and Jake felt a shiver go through him. It was not quite spring yet. In two weeks, the ponies would be brought home. He looked forward to seeing Chocolate and Lightning again. He missed them.

The End.

LETTER FROM PAUL BLADES

I hope that you have enjoyed the unfolding of the Maddy Saga as much as I have enjoyed writing it. If I tried your patience with diversions into the lives of the other characters, Jackie, the numerous slave girls, it was only to give a deeper, more resonate background to the general plot of the novel. Kalikastan seemed to me an extraordinary place and I wanted to fill in its various attributes in order to make my fantasy seem as real as possible.

I want to thank Agnes and Amy who provided me with wonderful covers to the books.

I also want to thank bdsmbooks.com for first publishing my work as e-books. I started out putting my fantasies on paper many years ago, but never thought of turning them into books until I received encouragement from Pentland, the former owner of the site. Simon, too has been encouraging and I thank him for all the kind words he has written about my work.

I doubt that I will ever go back to Kalikastan. I will miss the many characters, Jake and Maddy, Jackie, Klara, Antonia and poor little Amanda. Perhaps they will live on in your fantasies. Thank you for sharing them with me.

Paul Blades